Forgotten

Kent White

DEDICATED TO THE MEMORY of the eighty SOG reconnaissance team members who are still listed as MIA, including ten entire recon teams who vanished while on top-secret missions deep inside the jungles of South Vietnam, Laos, Cambodia, and North Vietnam between 1965 and 1972. You are not forgotten.

- AUTHOR'S NOTE -

DURING THE VIETNAM CONFLICT, communist North Vietnam used Laos and Cambodia, bordering South Vietnam to the west, as sanctuaries to harbor their troops and stockpile supplies for later attacks against US forces in the South. By late 1965, the US Air Force estimated some 30,000 North Vietnam Army troops were stationed throughout the region. Each month, an additional forty-five hundred NVA soldiers navigated the elaborate network of roads and trails located only miles from the South Vietnamese border.

As both Laos and Cambodia were declared "neutral" by the United Nations, the US military was forbidden to send in troops. While the 1st Air Calvary Division waged the first major battle of the war in October, 1965, in the Ia Drang Valley, a top secret Studies and Observation Group, or SOG, team comprised of two US Special Forces commandos and seven Nung hill tribe mercenaries infiltrated behind enemy lines into Laos to gather invaluable intelligence on North Vietnam's build-up. Thus began the first of hundreds of secret forays into Laos, Cambodia, and North Vietnam. These continued until early 1972 and were credited with saving thousands of American soldiers' lives.

On the 24th of April, 1969, B-52 bombers on a top-secret mission flew undetected over the mountains of southeastern Cambodia. Just before dawn, they unleashed their devastating payloads on a densely forested area of Cambodia, known as The Fishhook, where thousands of North Vietnamese Army troops were believed to be located.

Shortly after the bombing, a twelve-man SOG reconnaissance team took off in two 195th Aviation Huey helicopters from Quan Loi Airfield, a secret SOG launch site in South Vietnam, and infiltrated the area to make a BDA (Bomb Damage Assessment).

Comprised of five U.S. Army Special Forces' commandos and seven Montagnard hill tribe mercenaries, the recon team was accompanied by one of SOG's most notorious figures, Sergeant First Class Jerry Shriver. After more than three continuous years with SOG, Shriver's heroic and sometimes seemingly reckless exploits were known throughout the Special Forces' community, as well as the North Vietnamese Army. North Vietnam's Radio Hanoi honored him with the name "Mad Dog" and offered a ten thousand dollar reward for his capture, dead or alive.

Spotting a shell crater from the air, the Huey pilots believed they were in the correct target area. It was unknown to the men that the landing zone they were about to set down on had not received a B-52 strike and was surrounded by enemy soldiers. The instant the helicopters dropped off the team, a machine gun emplaced in a log-and-earth bunker raked the grassy LZ with a horrific maelstrom of automatic weapons fire, bringing down anyone who didn't find cover in the shell crater, or behind a charred tree trunk.

Shriver and another American, Walter Mercantel, leaped to the ground from the lead chopper as it hovered several feet above the LZ. Bullets snapped terrifyingly overhead. Instantly they fell to their bellies in the low grass. The withering fire tore away Mercantel's pack and canteen. Realizing there was little else they could do, Shriver led the mercenaries on a daring assault toward the tree line in an effort to silence the gun.

The other three Americans were in the second chopper and took refuge in the single shell crater. From his vantage point in the crater, Captain Paul Cahill watched in horror as he witnessed Shriver take several hits, then fall to the ground "like a sack of potatoes". A while later, the team's medic, Sergeant Ernest Jamison, sprang from the crater to aid a fallen Montagnard and was struck by a flurry of bullets and was killed.

Of the five Americans on the ill-fated BDA that spring morning, only two survived. Cahill, who was severely wounded and lost an eye, and Marcantel, who six months later died in a parachute jump at Fort Devens, Massachusetts. In one of their broadcasts, Radio Hanoi stated that Shriver had been captured. However, he has never been seen or heard from again and is still listed as MIA.

Whether he was captured and later killed, or died in captivity, no one knows, except perhaps the Vietnamese government. Some would like to believe he somehow escaped into the mountains and carried on his own private war with his beloved Montagnards, whom he was said to care more about than his American comrades.

There are ten cases of SOG recon teams, including twenty-five Americans, who went missing while on top-secret operations during the course of America's secret war in Cambodia, Laos, and North Vietnam. Their remains have never been found. A total of eighty SOG team members were lost. Their fate, too, remains unknown and many are still listed as MIA. They have largely been forgotten. This novel is about one such man.

I would like to thank Paul Cahill for assisting me in sorting fact from fiction about the events on that Cambodian hillside over forty-five years ago. I also want to thank Jim Morris and Write Monterey for ironing out the bumps.

Kent White

- PROLOGUE -

Fort Bragg, North Carolina
May, 1992

AT 0750, MASTER-SERGEANT Steven McShane, team sergeant for Operational Detachment A-115, ushered his team past a dour Military Policeman standing at parade rest by the compound gate. A persistent, icy wind clawed at McShane's exposed cheeks. He turned the collar of his field jacket up, to little effect. The cold numbed his skin. There was a half foot of snow beneath the pine trees from a freak, swift-moving Arctic snowstorm two days before. McShane hated the cold, and looked forward to the heated brick building.

The early morning briefing was held in 7th Special Forces Group's pre-deployment isolation center on Smoke Bomb Hill. The single-story isolation center was designed specifically as a secure site where operational detachments could plan top-secret missions. The center wasn't new to McShane: twice during the early days of the Gulf War, he and his detachment had spent several days planning covert operations into Iraq.

Surrounded by a ten-foot high chain link fence topped with coils of concertina wire, the structure had two stories. Only the upper story, which housed the administrative offices and classrooms, was visible. The lower story, where the mission briefings and operational planning took place, was located fifteen feet below the red-clay soil.

The nine other enlisted men and one officer assigned to the A-team filed hurriedly through the isolation center's steel door. They waited patiently inside the reception area, while another grim-faced MP checked their IDs, comparing the picture on the card to the holder's face. McShane quickly flashed his card, not caring if the ten-year-old picture looked like him or not, and went over to the window. He placed his hands palm down on the knee-high wall heater, and sat on them.

When the last ID was checked, the team filed down the formed concrete stairs and entered the sterile white cinder block briefing room. The rows of combination desks and chairs facing a large blackboard reminded McShane of a grade school classroom. The team sat in the first two rows.

The team members spoke quietly among themselves, speculating on the subject matter of the 0800 briefing. Hypotheses ranged from infiltrating the women's dorm at Chapel Hill to a HALO jump from 30,000 feet into Yugoslavia to train the Croatian militia. McShane didn't really care what the briefing was about. He was down to sixty days and a wake-up and he was finally warm.

Sitting in the front row next to First Lieutenant Alex Hansen, the team's acting commanding officer while Captain Briggs, their usual C.O., was on leave, McShane was about to ask Hansen if he'd scored with the nurse at the Officers Club the night before, when Lieutenant Colonel Frederick Shupp, 1st Battalion commander, and his staff, entered the room. The team immediately stood to attention.

"At ease, gentlemen," Shupp commanded.

In unison, McShane and his team sat down. Suddenly, as he settled into the hard metal chair, the room seemed hot and stuffy: he opened up his field jacket. Even Shupp seemed to notice the heat, dabbing his forehead with an OD handkerchief as he stepped toward the podium. His staff, including a civilian McShane didn't know, took their places on a row of folding chairs facing the team.

McShane tried to recall the number of briefings he had attended. It was impossible, but knowing that he was a week away from celebrating his twenty-seventh year in the Army, and guessing that he averaged one a month, he figured he'd sat in on at least three hundred, a nauseating thought.

Shupp stood behind the oak veneer podium with his hands locked behind his back. His intense blue eyes swept over the passive faces of the young team members. Except for McShane and Hansen, he suspected there wasn't a man over thirty. He wasn't misled by their ages, however. ODA-115 was the best operational detachment in the 1st Battalion, perhaps in all of 7th Group. He was proud of their accomplishments during his two years as battalion commander, including their work in Iraq before, during, and after the Persian Gulf War. Now he was about to assign them to another important mission.

"Gentlemen," he began, "you are, no doubt, aware of the recent rash of photographs appearing in various newspapers depicting alleged MIAs. While the majority of these photographs have proven to be clever forgeries, a few remain a mystery and are under intense investigation. Some photos received recently were kept out of the media's greedy liberal hands, and it is one such photo that prompted this briefing."

Shupp studied the young faces staring up at him. Their attention was riveted on his every word and he loved it. The power and control he had as battalion commander was invigorating. He was eager to see their expressions when they learned their assignment.

"At this point, I am going to turn the briefing over to Mr. Rayburn, a civilian asset, who will be your liaison throughout this operation."

McShane squirmed in his chair. Spook, he thought. The only civilians ever allowed at a classified briefing were with the CIA or DIA, or some other secret agency. He forgot about the heat. This was becoming interesting.

Rayburn was tall and athletically built. Sandy haired, tan, and dressed in L.L. Bean slacks and a blue Polo shirt, he looked more preppy than the slickly-dressed James Bond image of a secret agent. A graduate of Georgetown University, McShane thought, the college of choice for CIA recruiters.

"Good morning, gentlemen." Rayburn smiled warmly at the team. His teeth were white and even. McShane visualized him on a tennis court with a flaxen-haired beauty from Brown University, her well-rounded chest heaving from exertion. He didn't know whether to like this guy or not.

"Good morning, sir." The team retorted.

"Up until a few years ago, the Golden Triangle, specifically the remote jungle region of northern Thailand, southern Burma, and northeastern Laos, was the prime opium-producing area in southeast Asia. During the Vietnam War, the CIA used profits from the sale of the opium to finance covert operations throughout Southeast Asia."

McShane was surprised by Rayburn's revelation. He didn't think the CIA liked to discuss their drug-dealing days. But then, perhaps Rayburn had nothing to do with The Agency.

Rayburn moved from behind the podium and slowly paced the floor. "The Shan United Army, or SUA, is a private army originally formed in the mid-sixties by Khun Sa, an opium warlord. The SUA bought raw opium from hill tribe cultivators and sold it to Chinese syndicates in Bangkok. The syndicates, in turn, transformed the raw opium into heroin and sold it around the world.

"A lot of heat was placed on the SUA by Drug Enforcement Agency-financed Thai Border Police attacks in northern Thailand. The Border Police destroyed millions of dollars worth of poppy fields. Crop substitution, backed by the Thai government, replaced many of these former poppy fields with coffee, tea, and corn. Khun Sa and his army were driven into the mountains of the Kok River Valley in Burma. He still maintains a large army, for the protection of the Shan State, or so he says. More accurately, he still cultivates opium, but is less of a threat."

Rayburn paused and returned to the podium and consulted an open file. For a moment, he appeared deep in thought. He closed the file, rubbed his chin with the palm of his hand, and then turned back toward the team.

"With the SUA more or less out of the picture, the Laotians now run the smuggling operations. Backed by the Laotian People's Revolutionary Party, or the LPRP, Lao hill tribes are doubling their efforts to corner the market on opium poppies. It is still smuggled across the border into Thailand and sold to the same crime syndicates in Bangkok." Rayburn stepped from the podium and positioned himself directly in front of Hansen.

"For some time now, field operatives working inside Laos have known from their contacts with hill tribe growers, of armed Caucasians accompanying anti-communist rebels fighting LPRP forces. Our field operatives tracked some of these units and managed to take several photographs, confirming the existence of at least half-a-dozen Caucasians fighting with the rebel forces."

McShane was not aware that any of the sightings were actually confirmed.

"These rebels, interestingly, are remnants of the Special Forces trained FULRO, the Fronte Unife de Lutte des Races Opprimes. For those of you who have trouble with French, that translates into United Front for the Struggle of the Oppressed Races. The FULRO are comprised of several ethnic hill tribes, including the Mnongs, who were so loyal to SF during the Vietnam conflict."

And who we deserted in 1975, McShane thought bitterly, and who've fought every day since then to survive the oppressive Hanoi government.

"Through exhaustive background investigations, we discovered the identity of all these men. Two are former French Legionnaires, one is an ex-mercenary from South Africa, two are paroled Australian convicts, and one is a former Special Forces sergeant listed as MIA since July 1970."

A hush fell over the briefing room. McShane squirmed uneasily in his chair. This was all too familiar.

"We managed to keep close tabs on these men, particularly the American up until six months ago, when the sergeant vanished. Our contacts did a thorough search, and asked discrete questions of villagers, but nothing came of it.

"Last month, however, a story appeared in the Bangkok Post on the war between the KNU, the Karen hill tribe army, and the Burmese Army. Accompanying the article was a photograph taken near the northwestern Thai village of Naisoi. The photo shows a group of armed KNU guerillas filling their canteens at a stream. In the background, looking like a Western tourist with a camera slung around his neck, was our boy. This only came to our attention because one of our contacts, a hill tribe trekking guide, noticed the picture while waiting for a tour group to arrive at his hotel in Bangkok. He got a copy of the photo from the newspaper and turned it over to us."

Us who, McShane wondered? And what was the American now doing with the KNU, several hundred miles from the Golden Triangle?

"Frankly, we're baffled by his actions. Nobody knows why or what the sergeant was doing with FULRO or what the hell he is doing now with the KNU, some 300 kilometers from Laos. It seems he's helping the Karen, who have taken on the Burmese army in hope of creating their own state in southern Burma.

"So why does the sergeant care? Is he working as a mercenary, looking after his drug interests, sightseeing, what? More importantly, what has he been up to for the last twenty-two years? These are questions that need immediate answers. He needs to be found and brought out before somebody else recognizes him in the photo and starts blabbing to the press about him being an American MIA."

Rayburn returned to the podium and sipped water from a tall glass. "At this moment, political factions within the President's Senate Select Committee on POW/MIA Affairs are holding closed-door circle jerks, trying to decide what to do with stacks of reports on live sightings, and albums of photographs of purported MIAs. What we don't need, gentlemen, is the President's select few screwing this one up. Our man could die of old age by the time the committee members get their hands out of their crotches."

Rayburn focused his attention on McShane: "It is no coincidence that ODA-115 was chosen for this operation. Besides being the best team in the 7th, one of you here worked with the man in Vietnam, and hopefully will be able to positively identify him."

Before Rayburn even finished his sentence, the team guessed he was referring to their team sergeant, their only Vietnam vet. They studied him intently for a reaction. McShane remained poker faced, despite the stares.

"In every possible way, the man in the photo resembles existing military, private, and family photographs of Staff Sergeant Kevin Slade. Slade was the leader of Recon Team Utah, and a friend of Sergeant McShane, who led the Bright Light team into Laos to rescue Slade's team in July, 1970.

"As Sergeant McShane can attest, not one body was recovered from Slade's team. Four Americans and their indigenous interpreter simply vanished."

Rayburn held up the inch-thick manila folder he'd referred to earlier. Stamped across the front in red block letters were the words "TOP SECRET."

He crossed over to Hansen and handed him the file. "Lieutenant Hansen, your team will enter isolation at 1800 hours tomorrow, the 12th. This file is very thorough. There are maps, photographs, area assessments, intelligence data, politics of the region, known enemy strength, friendly assets, absolutely everything you need to prepare a successful operation.

"On the 16th, you will fly to Bangkok by military transport. From there, you will be flown by chartered aircraft to Chiang Mai in northwestern Thailand. There you will be met by your local contact, who will accompany you into the mountains. He knows the area, the hill tribes, and their dialects. He will assist you in final operational planning. The means of infiltration will be his responsibility also."

Rayburn paused to catch his breath. "I don't have to remind you how sensitive this mission is. Everyone out there, from the simple dirt farmer in Nebraska to the President of the United States, wants an accounting of the MIAs. Once you locate the man in the photo and verify his identity, you will hopefully learn the answer to our questions, and what happened to his team members. Were they killed, or captured and died during their captivity, or freed and simply chose to remain behind? If they chose to stay behind, we need to know why. Was it out of humiliation for what they revealed under interrogation, or because they felt a sense of duty to carry on the fight, or perhaps they wanted to make a buck with their former captors by dealing drugs?"

Rayburn suddenly glanced down at his watch and sighed. "Gentlemen, I'm out of time. Good luck." He turned abruptly on his heels and walked to the stairwell. One of Shupp's staff accompanied him out of the room.

Shupp rose quickly and went to the podium. "That concludes this briefing. Lieutenant Hansen, by 1730 hours tomorrow, your team will have all their detachment combat equipment packed. At 1800, you will be transported to this isolation facility, where you will begin planning your mission. Mr. Rayburn briefed my staff and they are available to answer any of your questions. Please let me remind you again of the sensitivity of this operation. Once you leave this building, you are not to discuss what was said today with anyone outside the team." Shupp extended his hand to Hansen, who stood and shook it.

"Good luck, Lieutenant Hansen.'

"Thank you, Sir.'

The battalion commander shook hands with the entire team before leaving the room, his staff on his heels.

Team members turned toward one another and began to whisper among themselves. McShane sat motionless. He was stunned that Slade might still be alive and fighting in Burma. What had become of him all these years? Were other Special Forces MIAs alive, choosing to remain behind rather than return to an uncaring society? There were too many unanswered questions. He needed a beer to help him sort things out.

McShane stepped behind the podium. "Okay, One-Five, let's cut the bullshit." He glanced at the wall clock across the room. It was 0830. "Team meeting at ten. We have a lot to go over before tomorrow."

Several of the team members groaned.

"At ease, girls," McShane said. "There will be plenty of time to wrap up last minute personal matters. When you explain where you'll be to wives, girlfriends, and boyfriends, use the same cover story we used when we deployed to Iraq."

The team hissed at McShane's boyfriend remark and began filing quietly out of the briefing room.

- C H A P T E R O N E -

Southeastern Laos
July 1970

BREATHING HARD, SLADE DUG his boot heels solidly into the mud bank. The earth was damp and slick, and his feet began to give way. He slung his CAR-15 automatic carbine over his shoulder and grabbed a low, overhanging branch jutting from a gnarled, silk cotton tree. With a swift yanking motion, he pulled himself up and out of the narrow ravine.

As he crested the slope, the branch snapped and Slade lost his footing, slipping in a pocket of mud left by the morning's monsoon deluge. His weapon slammed into his side as he fell to one knee. A jolt of pain tore through his rib cage. He barely managed to stifle a cry. Quickly recovering his balance, he brought his lanky six-one frame to an upright position. His blue-gray eyes took in the unfamiliar jungle, searching the dank depths for intruders.

Staff Sergeant Kevin Slade, Recon Team Utah's One-Zero, or team leader, had no idea how far they had traveled through the dense Laotian jungle. Often, they were only a few hundred meters in front of North Vietnamese Army trackers. They had already suffered one casualty, Cao, his point man, shot by an NVA soldier. His remaining four men were exhausted from being constantly on the move. Their water supply was at a crucially low point. If the team couldn't find a suitable site to take refuge and replace depleted body fluids, they would likely not survive the mission.

The thought of becoming added nutrients to the already rich, black jungle soil forced him to remain focused, and direct his energy on helping the remainder of his team negotiate the slippery hillside.

Sergeant Austin Broderick's legs pumped furiously as he tried to gain a foothold in the slick mud. At six-three and two hundred fifteen pounds, he was Utah's radio operator and One-One, and the largest team member. With the added weight of the PRC-25 radio riding high in his rucksack, he found the mushy bank a bitch to climb. His face twisted grimly as he struggled up the hillside.

Kneeling, Slade reached for Broderick's mud-caked hand, clawing frantically at the bank. "Grab my hand, Austin."

Broderick gripped the outstretched right hand and allowed Slade to half-drag him up the hill, while his feet churned in the quagmire, searching for a foothold.

"Fuckin' rain," Broderick muttered when he reached the top. He arched his back, then shrugged his shoulders to redistribute the awkward load in his rucksack.

"Quit whining," Slade commanded in a hushed tone. "There are people out there who want to screw up your day worse than a few raindrops. Give me a hand with the others."

Broderick's mud-smeared brow crinkled into a frown. For two-and-a-half hours, they had been dodging North Vietnamese Army patrols. So far, they had kept the NVA confused and at a distance, but all it took was one little screw-up to add the team to the ever-growing list of MIAs.

The embankment had become even more treacherous after Slade's and Broderick's knobby-soled jungle boots churned up the soil. Billy Mullins surveyed the bank for a handhold, a root, a rock, anything. He was a medic, not a mountain goat. Why had he let Slade lure him away from his regular job in the FOB dispensary?

"I'm short. Twenty-nine days and a wake-up," he'd told Slade three days ago when he visited him at the dispensary.

Slade had insisted. "One of my indig is sick and the other is at his dad's funeral and I don't have time to find replacements. Just this one mission."

Mullins had been content with his job, visiting local Montagnard villages, handing out malaria pills, performing physicals, giving inoculations, teaching villagers proper sanitation, and training the young 'yard nurses to care for their own people. Now he was wet and muddy, scared shitless, trying to climb what might as well have been Mount Everest.

Three feet up, Mullins discovered a thick, dinner-plate-sized rock uncovered by Broderick's boots. He brought his left leg up to the narrow stone ledge and carefully stood, testing the foothold. The granite chunk stayed securely embedded, and he brought the full weight of his body onto it. From this perch he gazed upwards. The distance had narrowed significantly, but he still remained out of reach.

Suddenly he felt his feet lifted from the rock surface. Glancing between his legs, he saw the top of Mark Lofton's red hair, wet and matted. Lofton, the team's One-Two, was nearly as large as Broderick and just as strong. His powerful arms gripped Mullins's thighs tightly as he pushed him up the embankment.

"Come on, you fat fucker," Lofton grunted. "Get your lard-ass up this hill before the NVA shoot it off." He gave Mullins a final shove then added, "and mine, too."

Billy Mullins and Mark Lofton had joined the Army on the buddy system out of Le Grand, a restless, run-down farming community in California's Central Valley. They had been friends since kindergarten, when Billy's parents moved from Carrollton, Alabama and bought a house next to Mark's on Jefferson Street.

Throughout high school, they were active in sports, co-captaining the football team in their junior and senior years. Their friendship strengthened during those years, and when an Army recruiter visited their senior class, and suggested they enlist on the buddy system, they jumped at the opportunity.

It was rare that the so-called buddy system kept a pair together much longer than Advanced Individual Training. But they remained together through Basic, AIT, Jump School, Special Forces Training Group, a brief stint as KPs with the 3rd Special Forces, and finally with the 5th Special Forces in Nha Trang, South

Vietnam. Eventually they were assigned to the same SOG FOB.

With the boost from Lofton, Slade and Broderick easily managed to drag Mullins to the crest of the embankment. When he reached the top, Mullins lost his footing and fell face first into a pool of brackish water. He jumped up instantly, choking and spitting. Despite their dire situation, it was difficult for them not to chuckle.

Mullins wasn't amused and swore to himself, wiping dark water from his face with his cravat. His stomach suddenly growled and he realized that a half-dozen bites of thawed, freeze-dried beef hash rations at daybreak was the last time he had eaten. When the others reached the top, perhaps they would have a chance to eat.

Lofton managed to scale the mud bank on his own, using the rock and some exposed roots uncovered by the others. Lap, their interpreter who was carrying the team's M-79 40mm grenade launcher, scampered easily up the muddy slope, following the precise route Lofton had taken. When they reached the top, Slade motioned them into a grove of Banyan trees.

The team hunkered down in the center of the trees and listened. Except for the thunderous pounding of Slade's heart and Broderick's labored breathing, it was quiet. For now, at least, it appeared they had eluded their trackers.

This was Slade's second tour with the covert, top-secret, Studies and Operations Group that operated deep in enemy denied territory. His first tour with SOG had been out of the FOB in Ban Me Thuot where he'd been a One-One, or assistant team leader, with Recon Team Beta, a nine-man team that generally operated in an area of Cambodia known as the Wastelands. When he was transferred to the FOB in Kontum after his 30-day extension leave, he was promoted to staff sergeant and given his own team.

He was now on the eighth month of his second tour, including two months recuperating in a hospital in Japan from a gunshot wound he received above his right knee while on an operation in southeastern Laos.

Slade blinked sweat from his eyes. He removed the coiled cravat tied around his head and wiped the mixture of water and perspiration from his face. He sat quietly against one of the trees, reflecting on the days' events. He was stinging from the loss of his point man, Cao, killed earlier in the day. He felt responsible for Cao's death.

Throughout his last tour in 1969, Cao had been on his old team, RT Beta, retiring when the team was disbanded. For the past year, Cao had been content puttering around the dilapidated stucco French Colonial house inherited from his father after the repatriation of Vietnam in 1954. Slade had worked hard to persuade Cao out of retirement. Finally, he relented, and agreed to join Slade's new team, RT Utah.

Cao had been walking point when the team entered what the SOG briefing officer, Captain Moses, had referred to as "strictly a deserted NVA bivouac camp." Moses was correct in calling it a "bivouac site", but deadly incorrect in the use of the word "deserted."

From the instant he and Cao set foot in the camp, Slade knew the intelligence was outdated. Signs of life were everywhere: an open cook fire boiling rancid water for drinking, tattered khaki uniforms hanging out to dry, and a sleeping soldier stretched out beneath a tree less than twenty meters from Cao.

Cao had responded instantly. With the muzzle of his M-16 trained on the slumbering soldier, he cautiously retraced his steps back into the dense jungle foliage, keeping the NVA keenly within the front sights of his weapon.

Cao's attention had been so riveted on the snoozing soldier that he failed to notice another NVA emerge from a nearby log-and-earthen bunker. Cao was within two steps of disappearing into the dull-green jungle when the soldier stopped abruptly, turned toward Cao, and knelt, bringing his AK-47 to his shoulder.

Slade had already stepped back into the foliage when he saw the NVA kneel and aim at Cao. He reached to grab Cao. But before he could grab his collar, there were two quick shots. Cao's head jerked back. A spray of dark red blood and jagged skull fragments erupted from the back of his head. He watched helplessly as Cao's body collapsed, an arm's reach away. There was no choice but to abandon Cao where he fell, with only half a head.

They'd made a hasty retreat toward their alternate LZ, taking only a brief rest for Broderick to radio the Covey pilot, Captain Jeffrey, who had been flying his single-engine Cessna 150 Birddog in their sector since shortly after dawn. He informed Jeffrey of their situation and requested immediate extraction. Jeffrey reluctantly replied that the gunships and extraction chopper were on a Bright Light rescue mission elsewhere.

That had been three hours before and Slade was worried there wouldn't be enough daylight for an extraction. He pulled out an acetate-covered map of their Area of Operations and spread it out before the team.

"We've got half the NVA in Laos looking for us," Slade began. "Fortunately, they don't have a clue where we are or where we're headed. Before they catch on, we need to get extracted." He turned toward Broderick. "Austin, get hold of Covey again. Forcefully explain the situation we're in, and that we need a ride out of here, ASAP."

With "Vietnamization" in full swing, support duties had been turned over to the Vietnamese Air Force. While their pilots were excellent, internal bickering among their commanders made them far from reliable. If their superiors felt their pilots had flown enough hours for the day, then they very well might decide to cancel their extraction. Slade worried that their air assets wouldn't arrive in time to get them out before dark, and he didn't relish the thought of spending another night in the Laotian jungle.

Broderick nodded, stood erect, and shrugged off his rucksack. Methodically, as he had on countless occasions, he unfastened the straps on the top of the pack, flipped the top flap out of the way, and turned the PRC-25 power switch to the "ON" position. The long antenna was broken down into a half-dozen lengths and stored in a two-foot-long canvas case. He pulled the sections out of the case, stuck them together, and screwed the end to the antenna mount on top of the radio. Lastly, he turned the knurled tuning knob until it clicked to the day's frequency.

"Billy, Mark," Slade continued, "I want you to set up a few meters out and make sure we aren't being tracked. Lap and I will plot out a course to the alternate LZ."

Mullins and Lofton nodded and moved to a low hedgerow ten meters to the south of the trees. Mullins settled in behind a tangle of deadfall and focused his attention toward the mud embankment. Lofton found a log partially hidden by swirling green vines, and took cover behind it. He rested his CAR on the log and scanned the dank jungle in the opposite direction.

Once Mullins and Lofton were in position, Slade returned to the map. It was an inaccurate rendering, compiled from maps drawn by the French in the 1940s and '50s. He studied the squiggly contour lines intently, attempting to get a fix on their precise location. He wondered just how inaccurate the map was. Their fate might well be decided by a French cartographer.

Slade tilted the map toward Lap. Lap knew the Laotian jungle better than anyone. He'd served with the French during the '40s and '50s as an interpreter and was familiar with their maps. If there were anyone in Southeast Asia who could direct them to the LZ, it was Lap.

"Say again, Desert Sun," Broderick said into the radio's handset.

"Repeat, Blackjack," Captain Jeffrey replied. "Lone Ranger is still down and won't be able to ride for twenty-four hours. Proceed to RON and continue with mission at first light. Out."

Broderick frowned, displeased with Jeffrey's message. He slowly re-fastened the radio handset to his web gear suspender, his team leader studying him. He hated to break the news to Slade.

"What, Austin?"

"Choppers are down for twenty-four hours. We're supposed to RON, then continue the mission. They'll try to extract us tomorrow."

Slade closed his eyes and sighed heavily. So much had changed since his last tour, when they still had the support of American pilots who would do whatever it took to extract a team. With the VNAF, there was always uncertainty. Good men would lose their lives from the VNAFs reluctance to fly. Well, before he would further endanger his men, he would lead them first to Thailand, two hundred kilometers due west, then to the nearest bar.

"Ain't this a batch of shit!" Slade muttered to himself, struggling to control his anger.

"What do you want to do?" Broderick asked.

"'Bout the only thing we can do. Find a place to hide out for the night. I doubt if the NVA have given up on us yet. They expect an exfil, and when they don't hear the Hueys, they'll know for sure we're still here.

And that will just intensify their search efforts. Get Mullins and Lofton over here."

He worried about the teams' chances of survival. In the last year, the NVA had become better armed. With their new man-portable SA-7 Grail anti-aircraft missiles, capable of bringing down a slow-moving Huey from ten kilometers out, teams were finding it nearly impossible to get in and out of AOs. Slade imagined an NVA weapons team lying in wait with dozens of Grails at the alternate LZ.

His dread was not unfounded. Last month, Eric Beck, his radio operator on several operations during his last tour, was killed along with his team when their Huey was hit on insertion by a Grail.

As a countermeasure, Slade had his team inserted several klicks from their destination, into an area not previously known for enemy activity. From the LZ, he had directed the team northwest, hacking through thick, nearly-impenetrable jungle in withering heat to reach their AO and the "deserted" camp. It had taken them two days.

His team had been assigned the mission of investigating the camp because of its close proximity to the village of Muong May, eight kilometers to the east of the village. Hypothesizing the camp had been abandoned, MACVSOG headquarters in Saigon hoped to use it as a staging point for a reconnaissance-in-force operation, code-named SLAM IX.

Muong May was a suspected NVA logistics complex, supplying enemy troops with weapons and food. Thirteen recon teams, each comprised of three

Special Forces men and nine hill tribe mercenaries, along with four companies of tribal guerrillas trained by U.S. Special Forces, were to take part.

The idea was nothing new. A bold plan by MACVSOG in March of 1967 had proposed that the hill tribes of the Annamite Mountains in southern Laos be organized into a guerrilla unit. They were to be outfitted and trained by Special Forces in Vietnam and then returned to Laos with SF advisors to fight against the Pathet Lao and the North Vietnamese.

In January, 1968, the plan was abandoned because of Embassy restrictions that forbade U.S. involvement in guerrilla operations within Laos. It was decided, instead, to recruit natives, train them in intelligence gathering in South Vietnam, and then return them to their homes in Laos to establish a network.

These agents reported that enemy activity in Muong May had increased dramatically and that the village was likely a major supply-and-staging point for NVA crossing into Vietnam. Now, nearly three years later, SOG decided to implement the plan once again. Muong May was to be the target of a massive B-52 bombing raid, immediately followed by an all-out assault by a recent, secretly CIA-trained force of hill tribesmen.

In addition to checking out the camp, RT Utah's mission was to recon the village of Muong May. Slade was to move his team into position near the village and place it under surveillance. They were to use whatever means possible to get in close enough to take pictures of any enemy build-up: stockpiles of weapons and ammunition, Grails, tanks, and soldiers with their personal equipment. In addition, they were to emplace electronic sensor devices to monitor troop movement on trails around the village. And, if the opportunity arose, they were to grab a prisoner. But, after the incident at the "deserted" camp, and with what seemed like every available NVA soldier in the area searching for them, Slade felt their mission had little chance for success.

When he got the team assembled, Slade reached for a foot-long twig to use as a pointer, slapping a thumbnail size mosquito on his left forearm. Flicking it into the brush, he pointed to the map.

"The choppers are down. Covey says they'll be out for twenty-four hours. However, since we're dealing with the VNAF, it could be longer." The faces around him tensed.

"It's too dangerous to hang out here, so I've decided we'll go ahead with the original mission." Lofton and Mullins's frowns deepened. "We'll proceed northeast toward the village of Muong May." He traced the approximate route with the twig. "That's about four klicks from here and will take us several hours. We'll RON somewhere en route.

"At first light, we'll proceed to the village and set up a staging point a couple hundred meters out. Lap and I will move to the village, check it out, take pictures, place some sensors, and return after an hour or so. At that time, I'll make a decision on how feasible a prisoner snatch is."

Slade surveyed his team members' distraught expressions. He gave them a wide, reassuring smile.

"Relax, I'm not about to place this team in any compromising situation. No dink prisoner is worth another team member's life. If it doesn't look good, we'll leave and wait for an extraction. Alright, let's go. We have a lot of ground to cover."

The team was up instantly. Slade rose slowly. The shoulder strap on his rucksack had worn his skin raw, causing him to wince as he stood. At twenty-eight, he often felt he was getting too old to be playing army, carrying a third of his body weight on his back like a pack mule, in an obscure country that nobody gave a shit about, and in a war that the people back home were fighting over more violently than the soldiers sent to fight in it. At the moment, none of it made any sense at all.

He held out his hand to Broderick, who was having a hard time standing up. The radio operator grasped it eagerly and with some effort, Slade pulled him upright. Again, a quick shrug of his shoulders shifted the bulky load on his back to a more comfortable position. Broderick managed a weak smile and gave his team leader a thumbs up.

Suddenly Slade's neck muscles tensed. He glanced back at Broderick. Broderick heard it too - a scampering noise from beyond the hedgerow. Slade motioned Mullins and Lofton to get down. They returned to their original positions near the hedgerow. At a crouch, Lap moved in the direction of the sounds to investigate, with Slade right behind him.

Slade heard the NVA clearly now. They were only a few dozen meters away, just on the other side of the hedgerow. Mullins and Lofton, their eyes wide and alert, shifted their bodies on the damp, musty earth, adjusting the aim of their CAR-15s toward the hedgerow.

Slade and Lap edged forward. They entered the thick knot of undergrowth, wriggling their way cautiously through the tangles of scrub brush. Slade parted some wait-a-minute vines and was startled by what he saw.

Less than an arm's reach away was a thin, well-worn trail. Slade inched forward to get a better look. He glanced first up the length of trail then down the twisting ribbon of brown muck. The trail was so enveloped in dense jungle vegetation that it was difficult to see where it began and where it ended. To his relief, the trail was clear of NVA. Apparently the soldiers they heard had already passed.

As he drew his head back, his attention was drawn to the center of the trail, and a small pocket notebook lying half-covered by jungle duff. Thinking the book might yield some valuable intelligence, he reached to pick it up. Abruptly, Lap grabbed his wrist and yanked his arm back just as a pair of tattered bata boots came into view. Slade watched helplessly as scores of NVA boots trampled the notebook into oblivion. Slade's heart sank as he grappled with the sobering realization of just how vulnerable his team was.

After the last of the soldiers passed, he motioned to Lap to move back. With the NVA trackers actively searching the immediate area, he knew they had to move quickly. Fortunately, the trail wandered off to the northwest. Muong May lay to the southeast. With any luck at all, their paths would never converge.

When they were out of the undergrowth, Slade pulled out his compass and checked their position. He pointed Lap to the southeast and moved in behind him. Broderick and Mullins followed Slade, and Lofton brought up the rear.

For the next forty-five minutes, they followed a narrow animal track that meandered along the military crest of a steep and rugged mountain slope. The sun began to drop behind the ridge. The mountain air turned cooler and less humid. Slade relished the change. In addition, the jungle had thinned, making their movement less restrictive and quieter. They were making excellent time now. It would be dark soon and he still needed to locate a suitable RON site.

Gradually, the track became uneven and slick. The team's progress slowed to avoid slipping. Even though Slade stopped them often to rest, the team grew weary with the slow, exhausting advance. Slade kept to the track, however, figuring the NVA were searching miles away.

As the track swung upward toward the crest of the ridge, the terrain changed abruptly. Before them lay an area unlike any they had covered the last few days. Tall, stout evergreen trees, like the forests of Oregon and Washington, covered the mountain slope. Lap, a half-dozen meters ahead of Slade, stopped.

When Slade caught up to Lap, he said matter-of-factly, "Looks like the Uwharrie." Lap looked at him curiously, not understanding Slade's reference to the

Uwharrie Forest in North Carolina, where Special Forces performed much of their local training.

"Maybe stay in trees?" Lap asked expectantly.

"Maybe." Slade motioned Lap ahead. There was little doubt the forest would be ideal for their purposes as long as it wasn't already occupied.

Lap stopped just inside the trees, moved off the track and knelt down. Slade signaled the others to take up a defensive posture off the path. They took cover behind some trees and trained their CARs on the wood line. Weapons poised, Lap and Slade cautiously entered the forest.

The thick evergreen forest made travel difficult. Slade and Lap squatted low to maneuver beneath some matted undergrowth clinging to the tree limbs. The air was still and cool. He felt as though he were discovering the forest for the first time. He slapped at a mosquito on the back of his neck. Apparently the forest had also been discovered by the Laotian bloodsuckers he'd come to detest long before.

They wandered deeper and deeper into the dark forest. Lap followed his instincts rather than any sort of path. With each step, Slade felt the strongest desire to turn back, yet he knew the forest was their only alternative. His men were exhausted and nearly out of water. The NVA were on to them and seemed to be everywhere, and this eerie haven offered the team immediate sanctuary.

- C H A P T E R   T W O -

TEN MINUTES INTO THE forest, they came to a broad, elliptical clearing. The grass-covered glade, thirty meters across at the widest point, was lit with a diffused late afternoon glow. Lap and Slade stayed in the shadows of the trees as they skirted cautiously around the outer edge of the clearing.

As inviting as the clearing appeared, Slade was leery of venturing into its warmth. It seemed too perfect, too serene to be real. The grassy meadow reminded Slade of the green coastal hills and meadows of the Central California coast between Carmel and Big Sur where he'd grown up. During the spring months, vast splotches of golden-cupped California poppies, dark lavender-petaled Blue Iris, and reddish-orange Indian Paintbrush covered the hills and meadows.

At the northeast edge of the clearing, they passed through a line of trees and into another, smaller glade. Slade figured the forest had once been bombed; intense heat scorched the jungle earth, causing long dormant grass seed to germinate. He stepped next to Lap who'd stopped before a tumbled mass of deadfall surrounding a massive teak tree. It towered above all other jungle foliage.

Slade was fascinated with the intricate network of twisting vines that clung tightly to broken limbs and smaller uprooted trees lying against the huge tree. Likely the result of vicious monsoon winds, he surmised. The mass of wooden debris formed a barricade two meters high and extended twice that distance out from the teak.

Slade prodded the brush with the muzzle of his CAR. It seemed impenetrable. He bent down and closely inspected the clutter of woven twigs, vines, and limbs, searching for a weak point. The deadfall looked similar to pictures he'd seen of beavers' nests. He parted some of the foliage and peered inside, half expecting a pair of foul smelling, yellow teeth to come snapping out at him. What he discovered instead was a pocket of open space about four feet high inside the dense thicket. Noticing some dry scat littering the floor of the wooden cavern, he hoped whatever critter had previously occupied the den wouldn't mind his team staying the night.

Slade stood. "Lap, get the team. We stay here tonight." Lap quickly disappeared into the trees.

Bending down again, Slade began shoving aside some of the deadfall to create an opening large enough for the team to crawl through. With a small tree branch, he brushed aside the dry scat. It'd be cramped for sure, he knew, but they would be safe until morning. Then the process of surviving another day would begin again.

Broderick was the first to arrive. Close behind were Mullins and Lofton. They stood before the wood entanglement, their eyes wide with amazement. Lap came up behind them, but stopped short of the clearing. He cocked his head slightly toward the way they had come, listening. The forest was deathly still. Satisfied they weren't being followed, he approached the deadfall.

Broderick helped Slade remove his rucksack. The relief from the burdensome weight was instantaneous. Slade rubbed his shoulders where the ruck's straps had dug in. The raw skin beneath his fatigue shirt stung from the sweat. Kneeling, he pushed the ruck through the opening and to the opposite end of the lair. Except for a meager amount of light filtering through the opening, it was ghastly dark inside. Sitting on the lumpy pack, he removed the crook-necked military issue flashlight from his web gear suspender and shined the narrow beam on the entrance.

"How the fuck did you ever find this rat hole?" Broderick asked as he forced his bulging ruck into the wooden chamber. "Goddamn, it smells like shit in here."

Slade snickered in the half-light. "Quit bitchin'. It's better than sleeping in an NVA bamboo cage."

Broderick moved his ruck next to Slade's. Lofton and Mullins quickly made their way into the room and sat next to Broderick. Mullins crinkled up his nose and sniffed. "Smells worse in here than my aunt's chicken house."

"I think Austin farted." Lofton added.

"Don't start with me, Mark. You can thank Kevin for the accommodations."

"Compared to the FOB latrine in the morning, this place smells like a floral shop," Slade countered.

Broderick looked at Slade and snickered. "Where do you get *your* flowers?"

Lofton and Mullins began to giggle. Slade ignored them and leaned forward, grabbing Lap's ruck as he pushed it through the opening. Lap, who had remained outside for one last lookout for enemy activity, entered the chamber and sat next to Lofton.

Slade motioned for them to quiet. While he realized the laughter was the first opportunity the team had had to release cooped-up tension, he didn't want them compromised, either. He reached into a side pocket of his ruck and pulled out two four-inch long white candles. He lit them with a single match from a box of Da Nang NCO Club matches. The room brightened instantly.

The team relaxed and drank conservatively from their canteens. Slade took a few sips and swished the tepid water around in his mouth. He savored the wetness, ignoring the bitter taste of the iodine-treated liquid. He could easily have consumed the half-empty canteen entirely in one long swallow. His throat was so dry that when he finally swallowed, it was as if he'd gulped air. He resisted the temptation to drink again. His remaining water would have to last until they could locate a mountain stream to refill their canteens.

Replacing his canteen, Slade looked over to Broderick. His features were indiscernible beneath the past day's dirt and grime. Broderick managed a weak smile.

"Austin, get a message off to Jeffrey. Tell him we're okay, tucked in for the night and will continue to the objective tomorrow." Broderick nodded and began to unpack the radio.

Slade glanced at Mullins and then Lofton. "Billy, Mark, I want you to find another way out of this forest.

I want to be able to get out of this place in a heartbeat if the NVA should luck out and find us. Don't wander off too far. It'll be dark in an hour. We'll go over the plans for tomorrow when you return." Mullins and Lofton nodded and crawled back out into the forest, taking only their web gear and CARs.

Slade spread his map on the ground next to the candles. Lap edged forward. Slade oriented the map to north and traced his forefinger from their last known location to the ridgeline they were on now. He studied it long and hard. Lap looked on curiously. There was no forest indicated on the map, Slade realized. Either the French cartographer was unaware of the forest when he drew the map twenty years earlier or he simply neglected to draw it in. Just a minor detail.

He found the village of Muong May and traced out a route the team could follow the next day. It crossed a narrow valley where he suspected they might find water. If they left at first light, they could arrive at the village by early afternoon, set up surveillance, take the pictures headquarters wanted and emplace the electronic sensor devices. If it looked promising, then perhaps the following day they could snatch an unwary NVA soldier and call for an extraction. They could be back at the club in time for happy hour. The thought brought a smile to Slade's chapped lips.

Lap watched the American closely. He didn't know what the team's mission was, but he sensed that it involved the village of Muong May. He remembered the village from the summer of '67 when he had led another Special Forces team there. At that time, it was just a small farming community. He wondered why they were returning.

"Sergeant Slade, I go Muong May maybe three years ago with Team Ohio. Very small village. Maybe ten huts, one-hundred people. Rice farmers. Some water buffalo, chickens, pigs. I know way to village."

Slade was startled by Lap's sudden revelations. It hadn't occurred to him to ask Lap what he knew of the area. He hadn't even disclosed the specifics of the mission to the others until the day before their insertion.

"Lap, do you know a good way to the village?"

The interpreter's brow furrowed as he shook his head, frowning. "From here, no easy way to village. Very thick jungle. Way you show on map maybe take seven, eight hour." He tapped the map with his forefinger. "Creek there. Beaucoup water." The place he indicated was at the base of a draw that emptied into the valley.

"Shit," Slade mumbled. He hadn't figured it'd take so long. Well, at least they'd be able to fill their canteens.

Lap gave his team leader a questioning look. "We go to Muong May?"

"Yes, tomorrow at first light. I'll tell the others when they come back."

Lap nodded approvingly then slid over to his ruck, leaving his team leader alone with his thoughts.

Broderick was bending the short-whip antenna back into his ruck when Mullins and Lofton suddenly entered the shelter. They were out of breath. Slade was anxious to find out from Broderick if he got through to Jeffrey.

But he also wanted to learn what Mullins and Lofton discovered.

"Well?" Slade asked Mullins.

"We followed an animal track east for about two hundred meters. At that point the forest ends and you're back in the jungle."

"Good. That's the way we'll go in the morning. Austin, did you get a hold of Covey?"

"Yeah. Jeffrey says he'll be back up in the morning around 0800."

"Perfect." Slade motioned the team to move in closer to the map. "Gather round. I'll go over the details of tomorrow's operation."

- CHAPTER THREE -

AT 0600 THE TEAM gathered their gear and followed the animal track discovered by Mullins and Lofton the previous evening. A cold mist clung to the forest floor, and persisted even as they left the tall trees behind and began descending the alien mountain slope to the lush valley below.

Broderick was relieved when they finally left the forest. He had slept fitfully the night before, plagued by a recurring dream of giant, snarling rats the size of men, dressed in NVA uniforms and armed with AK-47's. In each dream, the soldier-rats stormed their nest to rout the human intruders. Each time there was a firefight, and each time they drove the rats, their teeth as long and pointed as ice picks, from the forest. What he feared was that the vivid dreams were in some way predictions. The third time he had the dream he quietly crawled through the opening and sat outside against a tree until daybreak.

For the first few hours, the team traversed the mountain at an effortless pace, following animal tracks whenever they could. The remainder of the time they forged their own trail through the surprisingly light hillside foliage. A few minutes after 0900, Slade motioned the team into a bamboo thicket. He squatted against a thick, greenish-yellow stalk and pulled out his canteen. He jiggled it. There was a faint sloshing inside; it was nearly empty. At this point, he didn't care. They had to be close to water. He unscrewed the cap, tilted his head back, and sucked it dry.

"Is that all you've got?" Broderick asked, returning his own empty canteen to his web gear belt.

Slade nodded. "Yep, that's all she wrote." He held the canteen upside down, demonstrating that it was empty. "We'd better reach that spring or creek or whatever the fuck it's supposed to be soon, or I'm going to dry up like cow shit in the sun."

Broderick laughed softly. "I'm so thirsty right now that if I could take a leak I'd fill my canteen and drink it."

"Now that's thirsty."

Lap didn't bother to take a break, and went on ahead to search for the stream he was convinced was nearby. Lofton accompanied him. Mullins stayed behind and stretched out on a bed of bamboo leaves to rest while Broderick made radio contact with Captain Jeffery and informed him of their location.

He must have fallen asleep, because the next thing Mullins realized was someone shaking him. He bolted upright.

"Bad dream, Billy boy?" Lofton asked, grinning.

"Fuck off, Mark. Did you find any water?"

Lofton held up a canteen, unscrewed the top and placed it in Mullins' right hand. Without a word, Mullins tilted it to his lips and began gulping the chilled contents. He drank until he felt as though his stomach would erupt. With the canteen nearly empty, he handed it back to Lofton. Holding his stomach, he belched.

"That was better than a piece of ass, Mark. Where did you get it?"

"About three, maybe four-hundred meters south of here there's a waterfall that empties into a deep green pool of water. Looked like a scene out of a travel magazine. I thought a bare-breasted Tahitian nymph would step out of the waterfall and rip my clothes off. Wishful thinking, I know, but just to be on the safe side, I kept my eye on the waterfall while I was filling my canteens."

Mullins shook his head slowly. "You've lost it, Mark."

"Yeah, maybe so," Lofton said. "But wait, when you see that waterfall and the green water, you'll forget you're in Laos and someone's trying to smoke your ass."

"We'll see."

Slade overheard Lofton's conversation with Mullins. Lofton's casual attitude worried him. While he couldn't fault him for fantasizing a little, Lofton couldn't forget even for a moment where they were or the seriousness of their mission. The waterfall and the deep green pool could easily be flowing red with their blood.

Slade grabbed his arm and took him aside. "Listen carefully," he said sternly but low enough so the others couldn't hear. "This isn't a fuckin' game. You let your mind wander like that and you'll end up gettin' us killed." He paused a moment to let that sink in. "Lap spotted bata boot prints in the mud by the pool. Did you see them?"

Lofton's face flushed. He shook his head and stared at the ground, avoiding Slade's penetrating eyes. He was embarrassed that he'd been so careless, so preoccupied with adolescent dreams that he'd failed to notice the footprints. His team leader was right. He could have gotten them killed.

"I realize this is your first mission, so I'll cut you some slack this time. But if you fuck us up, I won't hesitate to shoot you myself. Understand?"

Lofton nodded.

Slade cracked the briefest of smiles. "All right then. Let's forget about your Tahitian princess and concentrate on gettin' through the operation and back to the FOB in one piece. Then I don't care who, or what you think about."

Lofton solemnly took his place next to Mullins. Neither said a word.

"We'll split up Lofton's and Lap's canteens with the rest of the team," Slade said to the team. "Maybe we'll find another creek further down in the valley. Right now, though, we have to hustle. I want to be in place by mid-afternoon."

The team picked up another animal track that switch-backed lazily through the jungle. For a change of pace, Slade took over point midway down the mountain. Up until then, their descent was effortless. But then it began to rain. The mountainside once again became slippery and treacherous. The nearer they came to the valley, the more closed-in the undergrowth felt. The air grew increasingly humid. Slade took every opportunity to stop and rest the team. While they were on something of a schedule, he didn't want his men too exhausted to effectively carry out their mission.

Shortly before noon, they reached the valley floor. Slade pushed aside some hanging wait-a-minute vines and stepped out onto a narrow, hard-packed road. He was startled to see two Laotian hill tribesmen dressed in brightly-colored loincloths. They were working a small green patch of rice paddy about fifty meters away. Slade quickly stepped back into the foliage and motioned the team down.

The Lao hill people unfortunate enough to be living in NVA-occupied territory were little more than slaves. Most served as porters, farmers, and guides. While the two men appeared harmless, their allegiance was to the North Vietnamese, if for no reason than fear for their own lives and those of their families.

The team studied the men and the surrounding paddy for the next fifteen minutes, using the down time to rest. Slade even managed to gag down a few mouthfuls of freeze-dried Squid and Rice LRRP rations left over from the night before.

Suddenly, something caught the Laotians' attention. They scurried out of the ankle-deep rice paddy muck and disappeared from view. Slade hurriedly closed up the foil LRRP packet and returned it to his ruck. Then, along with Lap, he low-crawled a little way out of the brush and into a drainage ditch paralleling the road to get a more unobstructed view.

Slade and Lap scanned the paddy and the surrounding area. There was no sign of the Laotians. A narrow, well-worn path running north and south cut through the middle of the paddy. Lap leaned close to Slade, and whispering in his ear, explained that the path continued to Muong May, less than a klick south. Slade guessed the Laotians had been summoned back to the village, perhaps by their NVA guard, who'd been dozing in the shade of a banana tree. They waited a couple of minutes, then low-crawled back into the jungle.

"Looks like we're closer to Muong May than I thought," Slade told the team. "Lap says it's just south of here. There's a trail that leads to it through the jungle. It's probably heavily traveled during the day. We'll keep an eye on it and see what we learn.

"This will be our staging point. There's good cover, good fields of fire, and in a pinch we can use the paddy as an LZ for an extraction. Lap and I will proceed to the village. Billy, Mark, keep an eye on that rice paddy and the trail. Note who comes and goes. Austin, radio Jeffrey, tell him where we are. He should be able to spot the paddy from the air. Once he identifies it, tell him to stay clear. I don't want the NVA wise to us." Broderick nodded and began unhooking the handset.

"We'll be gone at least a couple of hours," Slade continued. "Once we find the NVA encampment, we'll return and plan an action for tomorrow." Slade shrugged off his ruck. "We'll leave our shit here. If we're compromised and you hear small arms fire, call for an extraction. If we aren't back by the time the choppers arrive, go without us."

Without their rucks, Slade and Lap moved easily through the light jungle foliage. Lap's route paralleled the path. Every few minutes they stopped and listened. After a bit, they ventured out onto the trail and traveled along the hard pack. The trail, muddied from the earlier rains, was covered with boot prints. Two sets of bicycle wheel tracks etched the center of the path.

They followed the path for about half a klick when they suddenly heard voices. They quickly ducked back into the jungle and watched as the same two Laotians, accompanied by their NVA guard, sauntered toward the paddy. Slade and Lap kept to the jungle the remainder of the way to the village.

The village of Muong May straddled a narrow creek that meandered through the village. Slade and Lap hid in a stand of bamboo bordering the creek bank at the north end of the village. In appearance, Muong May was similar to the Rhade' village behind their FOB in Kontum. Twenty or so huts, constructed of woven bamboo, were built on teak poles three-to-four feet off the ground to keep them out of monsoon flooding.

For a moment, Slade watched several children playing what appeared to be a game of tag. He turned his attention to a group of Laotian men sitting in a semi-circle around a cook fire, talking quietly among themselves. Surprisingly, there was no sign of NVA activity. Slade tapped Lap on the shoulder and pointed out another stand of bamboo fifty meters south, indicating they'd take up position there.

They crept out of the bamboo and back into the jungle. As they moved cautiously through the undergrowth, Slade couldn't help wondering about the single soldier they saw on the trail with the Laotian farmers. It didn't make sense he'd be the only NVA in the village. No doubt, there was more to the village than the pastoral scene they just observed. The NVA, he had learned long before, were experts in the art of deception. He'd be a fool to think they would openly be wandering the village.

If an NVA logistical headquarters existed, it must be underground. The village quite likely had been taken over by the Pathet Lao and North Vietnamese for use as a decoy to throw off air reconnaissance. What he and Lap saw was what the NVA wanted them to see. From the air, he imagined the village appeared normal.

Slade and Lap bypassed the second stand of bamboo, opting to circumvent the entire village. Except for the children, the old men and a few elderly women weaving straw baskets, the village was deserted. From where they were, there was no indication of enemy activity. Not a weapon, vehicle, or even a uniform hanging out to dry. Nothing.

They broadened their search of the outlying jungle, moving further away from Muong May, but still circling the village. Slade felt that if there were a bunker complex, it would be located in close proximity to the huts. On their first trip around, Slade noticed a fairly wide trail at the southern edge of the village. This was the focus of his attention as they came around to the south again.

They located the hard-pack trail about two hundred meters from the hut where the women were weaving. Crouching low in a thicket of brush, Slade and Lap observed the trail for a few minutes. After a time, Slade ventured out onto the trail. He knelt down. Embedded in the wet clay were the impressions of scores of knobby-soled bata boots.

With so much apparent foot traffic, it would be suicidal to follow the trail. Slade stepped back into the brush and motioned Lap to continue south. They traveled alongside the trail for a while. He expected it to lead directly to an NVA encampment.

The undergrowth was so thick in places that they were forced to go around the entanglements. The detours ate up valuable time. They'd already been gone for the better part of an hour. If they didn't find something soon, Slade would return to the team, emplacing a couple of the sensors along the trail. Under the circumstances, it was the best they could do. Another team could be infiltrated if necessary, but he doubted it was worth risking any more lives.

Moments later they discovered another trail. Narrower than the first and not as heavily traveled, it intersected the other in an east-west direction. Slade stood just off to the side of the new trail and opened an ammo pouch. He pulled one of the electronic sensors from the bag.

The sensors were designed to register body heat and vibrations. The information was transmitted north via satellite to the National Security Agency in Hue City, where it was analyzed by intelligence experts. From this data, they determined how many people walked up and down the trail during a given time.

A light rain began to fall. Slade hurriedly unfolded the sensor's spiked legs and stuck it just inside some brush at the northeast corner of the trails. He activated it with a flick of a toggle switch on the side of the battery-operated unit. He carefully camouflaged the sensor with some dry leaves and twigs. Satisfied the device was undetectable, he led Lap across the trail and back into the jungle.

Suddenly, a flicker of hazy movement about twenty meters ahead caught Slade's eye. He signaled for Lap to get down. They both crouched beside a man-size tree fern. They trained their attention on the blurred form of an NVA soldier moving toward them. They raised their weapons simultaneously.

The soldier paused about a dozen meters from their position. Slade sighted his CAR on the NVA's chest. It would be a sure, lethal hit from that distance, but one he didn't want to risk taking. Killing the soldier would create a shitstorm of such intensity that getting out of Laos alive would be a real test. He breathed slowly, quietly, waiting anxiously for the soldier to make a move.

Then another NVA popped out of the jungle underbrush, catching Slade off guard. He was joined by a third, then a fourth. Within moments, six more were added. Slade was baffled. They seemingly materialized out of nowhere. He kept his gaze locked on the squad-size group of soldiers, curious as to where they came from and what they were up to.

The first soldier conversed in harsh tones with the others then led them single file toward the trail. As quickly as they appeared, they vanished in the rainy haze. Slade looked to Lap for an explanation.

Lap leaned close to his team leader. "Soldier their squad leader. New recruits. They fuck-ups. He tell them they clean out shit holes. Maybe after, they not be fuck-ups."

Slade nearly laughed out loud. Soldiers were soldiers, regardless of politics. Somewhere in Vietnam, Slade mused, American soldiers were doing exactly the same.

He glanced at his watch. They had to get back. He'd seen enough to warrant another visit tomorrow. But before they returned, he wanted to make at least a preliminary investigation of the area where the soldiers suddenly appeared. He figured there was probably a spider cave or a camouflaged bunker cleverly concealed beneath the jungle flora.

They advanced slowly, at a half crouch. Slade held his CAR steady on the grove of tree ferns where the soldiers had been. With his back to Slade, Lap swept his eyes suspiciously over every fern, tree and bush. A couple of meters away, Slade knelt. He eased to his belly and slithered into the ferns. Lap held back, protecting his rear.

It came as no real surprise when Slade low-crawled out of the ferns and discovered an expertly hidden, meter-square opening to an underground bunker. Slade hesitated a moment, deciding whether or not to approach the log-framed entrance. For a fleeting moment, he considered entering the bunker, but immediately realized the insanity of this.

To his left, fronting a muddy trail, were the entrances to at least six other bunkers. It required a great deal of mental and physical restraint to keep from lobbing a grenade or two into each of the bunkers. But that wasn't their mission, he reminded himself. He would have to be satisfied with emplacing the remaining sensor and returning tomorrow with a full team.

He placed his last sensor under some jungle duff among the tree ferns near the first bunker entrance, and crawled out of the grove. They retraced their steps back to where they first saw the soldiers. Slade pulled his compass from his top right pocket and shot a more direct azimuth back to the paddy. Now that he knew where the NVA camp was hidden, it wasn't necessary to follow the trail back to the village.

The southwesterly course took less than thirty minutes to complete. Slade found the team spread out along a ten-meter stretch of the tree line, intently studying the rice paddy. Curious, Slade crouched next to Lofton and peered through the brush. Stooped over a row of new green shoots were eight bare-breasted teenage hill tribe girls. Slade shook his head, chuckling quietly, as he reached for his canteen.

"We'll RON inside the jungle tonight," Slade said. "That way we can be close enough to the trail to monitor enemy movement. That doesn't mean, however, that we're here to study boobs. Now let's move farther back into the jungle, and find someplace where we can hide out for the night."

- CHAPTER FOUR -

SLADE MOVED THE TEAM out just before dawn. They followed the same general route he and Lap had taken on their return the afternoon before. A dense mist hugged the ground, reminding Slade of the dry ice fog in a 1950's "B" horror movie. The chilled air was invigorating; he felt renewed strength as he followed Lap on a steady, but unhurried pace through the forest.

Mid-way to their objective, Lap heard voices coming from beyond the trees. Recognizing the voices as Laotian, Lap figured it was a hunting party or some farmers getting an early start. The team kept a close eye on the forest as they turned away from the village on a due north heading. Once they were out of earshot, Lap picked up the pace.

A half-klick later, Lap changed direction again and led the team back toward Muong May, cutting west through a dense thicket of tangled brush and wait-a-minute vines. Slade was thankful it was still cool.

It took them the better part of an hour to negotiate the thick underbrush as they tried to maintain their stealth. When they emerged from the thicket, they were within sight of the stand of bamboo where he and Lap had first observed the village. The team eased to a crouch and crept cautiously toward the bamboo.

Slade signaled for the team to spread out along the stout shoots. He figured they would keep the village under surveillance for a while and then leave Mullins and Lofton with the half-frame Olympus Pen camera while he took Lap and Broderick back to the bunkers.

After half an hour, the only visible activity was three old women gathering water from the well, while two little boys scampered after a bright green lizard. Slade was curious about the lack of village life. The Montagnard village behind their FOB usually bristled with activity this early in the day. He suspected the villagers, little more than slave laborers, had already been rounded up by the NVA and taken out to the fields.

Slade edged closer to Broderick, who was stretched out on his stomach with his chin resting in his hands, watching the kids. Broderick turned toward him and smiled.

"Come on," Slade said. "Let's check out the bunkers." Broderick nodded and rose slowly.

On their way out of the bamboo, Slade pulled Lofton and Mullins aside. "You're on your own. If the bad guys show up get plenty of pictures. We'll rendezvous here in two hours."

Slade and Broderick followed closely behind Lap as he led them toward the bunkers. Slade was curious to know just how far the complex extended into the jungle. As they approached the encampment from the south, they came to a chest-high hedgerow. Voices could be heard in the distance. They crouched down and peered through the scrub brush. Dozens of NVA soldiers were seated at three long wooden tables eating rice from clay bowls.

A column of soldiers holding empty bowls stood patiently a few feet away, waiting to be served from a huge cast iron pot. As a table of soldiers finished, they were replaced by the soldiers in line. In the two or three minutes they observed them, Slade counted thirty NVA come and go. Soldiers steadily arrived in groups of ten.

Slade had brought along his own personal camera, a Pentax Spotmatic. He often took pictures of his own in the bush. However, because of the Pentax's noisy shutter, he normally stuck to S-2's quieter Olympus Pen half-frame when taking pictures of the enemy. But this was too great an opportunity to ignore. Never had he seen so many NVA concentrated in one place. Besides, he was confident the soldiers' chatter would drown out the shutter's clicking sound.

In slow succession, he snapped off three pictures, pausing between each shot to observe the soldiers' reaction. After the first three pictures went unnoticed, he took another half-dozen, focusing on two Chinese manufactured trucks parked alongside the mess hall, as well as a row of bunkers thirty meters to the west, from which several soldiers entered. As soon as he and Lap rejoined the others he would get Broderick to radio in the map grid coordinates for a B-52 strike.

Satisfied he had what he wanted, he motioned Lap to continue along the hedgerow. The clump of brush extended another fifty meters and then ended abruptly at a trail that cut east to west. They followed the brush to the trail, hesitated a moment to check it out, then crossed. Within moments they were hopelessly bogged down in a dense thicket of underbrush. It was impossible to move quietly, so he motioned Broderick and Lap back toward the trail.

As Slade stepped out onto the trail, a sudden motion caught his attention. His jaw dropped when he turned to look. Two soldiers on bicycles were pedaling toward him. Locked in conversation, the NVA were at first unaware of his presence, but before Slade could double back, one of the soldiers spotted him. "Fuck!" Slade muttered. He stood his ground in the middle of the trail and waited.

The startled soldiers braked and swerved to get around Slade. Slade grabbed the closest soldier by the collar and yanked him off the bike. He twisted the NVA soldier's arm up and behind his back, forcing his face into the mud.

Lap and Broderick surrounded the other NVA. Lap drew his M-16 back and crushed the butt of the weapon into the side of the soldier's skull. The soldier's foot became entangled in the wheel spokes and the bike flipped, hurling the soldier along with the bicycle into the hedgerow.

Afraid the sound of the soldier and bicycle crashing into the hedgerow might bring more soldiers from the camp, Broderick dashed into the hedgerow. He hurriedly jerked the dead soldier's leg from the wheel, threw him over his shoulder, and carried him across the trail and into the jungle. Lap pulled the wrecked bike into the jungle, then darted out once again and dragged the other soldier's bike off the trail.

Slade quickly blindfolded and gagged his captive while Lap handcuffed him. Broderick dropped the dead

NVA into a shallow depression a couple meters inside the jungle. He scattered twigs and branches over the body. When he returned, Lap had already camouflaged the bicycles with brush. Slade crouched next to the POW who was face first in the damp ground.

"Broderick, get on that fuckin' radio and call for an extraction."

"Where?"

Good question, Slade thought. Their primary and alternate LZs were out of the question; the NVA would go there first, as well as any other probable LZ. Maybe they could move into the jungle and find a suitable site for a McGuire rig extraction. But that could take too much time. Damn, why did those two idiots on bicycles have to fuck up his plans? Only one location came to mind.

"The rice paddy. We'll take cover in the old shell crater we spotted earlier."

While Broderick tried to raise Captain Jeffrey, Slade thought about what to do with the prisoner. He lie motionless on his stomach. There was a faint odor of urine. He thought for sure it was the NVA's, but checked his own pants to be sure. They were dry. Good, he thought. He didn't want it to get around that he had pissed his pants.

If the soldier caused them any trouble, he would kill him. They couldn't risk that he might warn his comrades. Whatever he knew about the bunker complex was less important than the team getting out alive.

Broderick refastened the handset on his web gear suspender and flashed his team leader a broad smile.

"They're puttin' together a Bright Light team. FOB scrounged some American pilots from the 4th Division. They're bringing two Cobra gunships."

"Good. We'll need 'em. This will be one hell of a hot LZ. Hopefully, we'll have the element of surprise on our side. Let's get back to Billy and Mark." Slade jerked the POW to his feet. Keeping a tight grip on the soldier's left bicep, he guided him through the foliage toward the trail. He noticed the crotch of the soldier's pants was wet.

Broderick crossed the trail first, while Slade and Lap waited just inside the brush line. Suddenly, four soldiers came running down the path, their weapons at the ready. One of them spotted Broderick just as he crossed the trail, and shouted a warning to the others. In unison they stopped and raised their AKs.

Slade momentarily released his hold on the POW and fired a quick burst, dropping two of the soldiers where they stood. Lap shot another soldier in the chest and the remaining NVA with a round to the neck. The prisoner started to run, but Slade grabbed his arm again.

There was no question in Slade's mind about what to do with the prisoner. With their own safety in jeopardy, they couldn't be hindered with extra baggage. Without hesitation, Slade pressed the soldier's face firmly into the mud, removed his Marine K-bar from its sheath and jammed it into the side of his neck, splitting the jugular in two. Bright arterial blood spewed onto the trail. The prisoner's neck was nearly severed when he yanked the knife out.

Slade led them back along the hedgerow. Even though it passed directly in front of the bunker complex, it was the quickest and most direct route. He suspected the NVA were probably in a state of confusion at hearing the gunfire. Hopefully, he thought, they would be reluctant to charge out into the jungle blindly without first assessing the situation. He wanted to get back to Lofton and Mullins before the NVA figured out what was going on.

* * *

Startled by the gunfire, Lofton and Mullins tightened the grip on their weapons and peered through the bamboo. They knew the mission had now been compromised, and it wouldn't be long before the surrounding jungle would be crawling with NVA.

Suddenly, a number of NVA showed up in the village, and began shouting at the few villagers present. More villagers scurried from the bamboo longhouses and lined up in loose formation. Lofton was mystified. He had assumed Muong May was deserted. He never guessed that everyone was restricted to their homes.

Lofton shifted his gaze from the village to the thick jungle vegetation on his right. Several North Vietnamese soldiers moved among the trees. They methodically swept the forest, prodding the undergrowth with the tip of their AKs. Lofton fought back panic. The NVA were quickly closing in on him and Mullins.

"Shit!" Mullins whispered. "The NVA are all around us." NVA from Muong May now scrambled across the narrow stream and moved into the bamboo forest.

"We're screwed," Lofton muttered. They were trapped. The soldiers would be upon them any moment. He reached down and flicked his CAR's selector switch from semi to full-automatic and took a grenade from his web gear suspender. Well, he decided, they would give the NVA a hell of a demonstration of American firepower.

Mullins followed Lofton's actions. "Let's split for the trees behind the village before they get out of the bamboo," Mullins suggested. "They'll never expect us to run through the village. We'll backtrack and meet the others back at the paddy."

They crept to the edge of the woodline and scanned the open jungle. The village was empty now. The villagers had either retreated back into their homes or were helping the NVA search. They heard hacking as the soldiers cut a swath through the bamboo forest.

"Let's do it, buddy," Mullins said.

At a crouch, they lunged from their concealed position and sprinted through the open forest, ignoring brambles and branches. They headed toward the south end of the village where they had first seen the kids playing tag. As they neared the stand of bamboo, they noticed the tops of the stalks swaying. They could hear the soldiers hacking furiously at the shoots with broad knives.

Leaping the creek, they zigzagged across the open space between the two longhouses and dived beneath a small hut. They hid behind a score of tall, cylindrical woven bamboo baskets filled with rice. Suddenly, a scurry of footsteps drew their attention to the longhouse next to them. Three NVA came bounding down the bamboo ladder-stairs. They pressed their bodies into the damp soil.

At the base of the stairs, the NVA paused and scanned the village. Lofton sneaked a peek between the baskets. From their animated gestures and rapid-fire speech, he guessed the soldiers had heard them, or at least thought they had. Exchanging puzzled looks, the NVA fanned out, cautiously approaching the longhouse across from them.

The North Vietnamese started their search among some small wooden crates and boxes stored beneath the thatched structure. Two soldiers probed with the tips of their AKs, while the third stood off to the side, keeping watch. Mullins and Lofton watched the two soldiers as they methodically went from box to box. They exchanged quizzical looks and tried not to laugh. How in hell, they wondered, did the soldiers think they could cram their bodies into such a confined space?

When the two NVA finished with the last of the boxes, the soldier standing watch shouted to them. They quickly moved to his side. They spoke quietly among themselves. Suddenly they turned and approached the hut where they were hiding.

They waited until the soldiers were nearly upon them then burst from their concealed position, leveling their weapons on the three soldiers. They opened fire simultaneously. The soldiers spun backwards and collapsed.

Mullins and Lofton sprinted toward the tree line behind the hut. They maneuvered a hundred meters north into the vegetation, and then ducked inside a dense pocket of brambles. They knelt and listened. Chaotic shouts echoed throughout the forest. Mullins and Lofton turned toward one another and grinned. They'd outsmarted the hangman, at least for the moment.

Before the soldiers could organize a search party, Mullins and Lofton were again on the move. They traveled another two hundred meters north, and then swung in a large arc and headed back toward the paddy. As they paralleled the village, they heard a gravel-voiced soldier barking orders in Vietnamese. They hurried through the forest, anxious to put as much distance as they could between them and their enemies.

As they came back around to the trail that ran to the paddy, they heard gunfire erupt from the direction of Muong May. They paused to listen. The sharp report of measured, semi-automatic M-16 fire was interspersed with volleys of full automatic AK-47 fire. Mullins judged the NVA had been caught off guard by Slade, Broderick, and Lap.

"Let's get us some," Mullins said. They struck off toward the sounds of gunfire.

They met Slade and Broderick a few minutes later, huddled in a dense grove of trees. Lap was conspicuously absent and Broderick was limping. There was a large patch of blood just above his left knee. He grimaced as he staggered toward Mullins.

Mullins pulled his aid-bag from his rucksack, and sat Broderick down against a tree. He hurriedly ripped open his pants. Blood pumped slowly from a puffy entrance wound the size of his thumb. Mullins tore the foil wrapping from a field dressing and bound it tightly around the hole, tying it off in one swift motion. Slade knelt down beside him and handed Broderick his canteen. He took a couple swallows.

"I see you got yourself a million dollar wound, Austin," Slade said, smiling reassuringly. "Worth at least a month in Japan."

Broderick winced as he rose to his feet. "If we get out of here."

"Never let you down before, have I, buddy?"

"Guess not."

Mullins grabbed Broderick around the waist to steady him. "What happened out there?" Mullins asked.

"We butted heads with a platoon of pissed-off dinks," Slade explained. "Luckily, we saw them first. Managed to catch them off guard and scattered them before they could do too much damage."

"Where's Lap?"

"Don't know," Slade said. "He went screeching after the NVA, firing like a madman. The NVA probably thought he was a forest devil or somethin.' Those soldiers must be scattered all over Laos by now. If it hadn't been for him, we'd be history. He saved our asses for sure."

Slade took the radio out of Broderick's rucksack and squeezed it into Mullin's rucksack. Lofton removed the Claymores then rigged a grenade beneath Broderick's ruck to detonate if it was picked up.

The team headed toward the paddy. Lofton took point, with Broderick following directly behind. Broderick was limping. Mullins stayed close behind, to be there if Broderick needed assistance. Slade held back several meters to cover their rear. It was only a matter of time before the platoon they'd chased off was replaced by even more NVA, all bent on revenge. Slade prayed the Bright Light team would arrive soon.

A few hundred meters from the paddy, Broderick's knee gave out. He cried out softly. Mullins reached forward to steady him, placing his left arm around his waist.

"Son-of-a-bitch," Broderick groaned. "Think the kneecap popped loose or something. Got to sit down."

"Shit, Austin, we can't right now," Mullins pleaded. "We're almost there. I made reservations at the NCO Club. They're stocking up the coolers with cases of beer. Just for us. Free, too."

Broderick managed a weak smile and for a time Mullins managed to keep his friend's mind off the knee with words of encouragement, reminding him repeatedly of the free beer. But after another difficult hundred meters through some dense vegetation, his leg buckled again.

Lofton heard Broderick cry out and pulled back. Slade came up from the rear. One look and he became immediately concerned about Broderick's condition. His face was pale and drenched in perspiration. The field dressing was soaked through.

"Get him down, Billy," Slade ordered. Mullins lowered him to the ground and set him against a log. He offered Broderick his canteen. Broderick gulped a half-dozen swallows.

Slade turned to Lofton and spoke quietly. "I heard NVA trackers. They're only a few hundred meters behind us. Austin looks like shit and he can't walk. We're going to have to carry him."

Lofton nodded. "Billy can take point. I'll carry Austin."

"I'll relieve you in ten minutes," Slade said.

As Lofton helped Broderick stand, Slade heard rustling in the trees thirty meters to their left flank. He brought his CAR to his shoulder and pointed the muzzle toward the sound. Lofton slowly lowered Broderick behind the log and took cover next to him. Mullins ducked behind a tree. Suddenly, two NVA soldiers stepped out into the open. They hadn't seen the team.

Slade kept his front sights trained on the soldiers as they advanced toward them. His heart raced. He stood motionless, incredulous that the soldiers hadn't spotted him standing in the open. He kept the soldier on his left clearly within his sights. He would take him out first, but he prayed it wouldn't be necessary. Their shit was weak enough as it was.

A dozen meters away, the soldier-on-the-left's gaze shifted and locked on Slade's cold, level glare. The soldier's jaw dropped. An expression of utter horror spread over the NVA's face. He fumbled for the selector switch. Slade felt a moment of sorrow for the kid. He hated to kill him without at least offering him the chance to get his weapon off safety.

"Fuck him," Slade mouthed. He fired a single shot into the soldier's throat. Mullins, who had been following the progress of the soldier on the right, shot him twice in the chest.

Lofton quickly eased Broderick, who'd passed out from loss of blood, over his shoulder. The dead weight of Broderick's body caused him to stumble, but he quickly regained his balance and followed Mullins toward the paddy.

Slade took up a defensive position behind a tree and scanned the jungle. The two soldiers, he was sure, had been the point element for a larger NVA search party. If they showed up he'd be able to hold them off for a while, allowing the team time to reach the rendezvous site. He would catch up later.

The team was out of sight when a soldier cautiously poked his head out of the trees and studied the bodies of his fallen comrades. He raised an arm and made a signaling motion. Soon he was joined by ten others. They spread out and advanced cautiously toward the two dead men. The soldier who signaled the others knelt beside the one Slade had killed. He took the dead soldier's canvas ammunition pouch, then moved to the other body and retrieved his, too.

Slade watched him with interest. Ammo was a valuable commodity to the NVA. He mentally applauded their "waste not, want not" approach. Too bad he had to waste them.

He opened up with a series of three round bursts, working on the file of soldiers from left to right. He managed to disable the first five before the others could react. He hurriedly replaced his magazine. When the remaining NVA began to disperse, he took them out one by one. Only the soldier who had knelt to collect the pouches managed to avoid the initial onslaught.

That soldier dropped behind the body of his fallen comrade and returned fire. Like a snapping turtle retreating into his shell, Slade pulled himself back behind the tree. A steady barrage of AK rounds chipped away the bark. Then he heard the AK's bolt snap closed.

Overeager, the soldier had emptied his thirty-round magazine in a single burst. Slade took advantage of the soldier's lack of discipline and popped around the tree.

The NVA frantically fumbled to reload another magazine. Slade shifted his position to another tree five meters to the soldier's right front for a clearer field of fire. He rested the muzzle of his CAR on a leafy branch.

Slade could see perspiration drip from the youth's brow as he fixed his sights on the red star just above the brim of his pith helmet. The soldier suddenly shifted position, taking cover behind his comrade's corpse. Slade realigned his sights on the soldier's left ear. He could make out a pair of flies buzzing around the lobe. He wondered if he'd get the soldier and flies all in one shot.

An eerie quiet had fallen over the jungle forest. Slade felt the rhythmic thump of each heartbeat. He breathed slowly, methodically, calmly. The soldier's ear seemed to loom larger than normal as he tightened his pull on the trigger. The flies had now crawled onto his lobe. He was so focused on the soldier's ear he failed to hear the twig snap behind him.

* * *

Private Nguyen was still fumbling with the magazine when he heard the shot. Instinctively, he ducked down behind the corpse of his fallen comrade. A second shot rang out. For the first time that day he smiled. The two shots were not from the American's weapon, but from one of their own. He glanced furtively over the cadaver. Suddenly, five men from his platoon emerged from the foliage. Nguyen stood and approached his comrades. Together, they gathered around their fallen foe, grinning. They spoke quietly among themselves, amazed at his size and blond hair.

Sergeant Tran, their platoon leader, knelt beside the American and turned him onto his back. The enemy soldier's vacant eyes were fixed upward. They blinked once and seemed to try to focus on Tran. He licked his chapped lips. Tran lifted the enemy soldier's head and gave him some water. The American drank eagerly and Tran felt an immense respect for this soldier who had unselfishly remained behind so that his comrades could reach safety.

* * *

Mullins and Lofton had crossed the trail to the paddy when they heard the gunfire from Slade's CAR-15, and then moments later two single AK shots, followed by silence. Worried, Mullins hurriedly lowered Broderick to the damp jungle duff. He took the radio handset and called Covey. Jeffrey's clear baritone voice replied almost immediately.

"Go ahead, Lone Ranger."

"Need an extraction ASAP. Enemy all around us. One WIA. Two MIA." Mullins didn't know positively if Slade was MIA, but the two unanswered AK shots worried him. He'd rather believe he was MIA than KIA.

There was an annoyingly long pause. Mullins held the handset away from his ear to avoid the irritating cackle of static.

"Roger, Lone Ranger," Jeffrey finally said. "Launch site has a Bright Light team on standby. Waiting for gunships to arrive. Just hold tight, buddy. You're as good as home."

Mullins wished he could be as optimistic. First they'd lost Cao, then Lap went missing, Broderick's wounded, and now Slade's missing. Out of a six-man RT, he and Lofton were the only ones capable of putting up a fight. And they were supposed to "just hold tight"? It was a good thirty minutes of flight time from the launch site. And they hadn't even left yet.

Lofton stood behind a tree a few meters away, his CAR pointed in the direction of the gunshots. His concentration was focused on a narrow clearing between a dense thicket of snarled vegetation thirty meters ahead. He suspected the NVA would likely come at them through there. One automatic weapon wasn't much, but he figured he could hold off a substantial force for a time while Mullins carried Broderick to a shell crater at the south end of the rice paddy. He turned slightly when Mullins approached, not wanting to take his eyes completely off the clearing.

"Jeffrey says Bright Light team should be on the way soon," Mullins whispered.

Lofton nodded. "You take Broderick to the crater across the way. Like Slade figured, they likely won't be looking for us there. I'll stay for a while and hold them off if necessary. Leave the radio. I'll notify Jeffrey and then join you."

Mullins nodded. Lofton helped Broderick, who'd passed out, to his feet, then onto Mullin's back. The dead weight bearing down on Mullin's back pushed his legs to their breaking point. He struck out toward the crater, thinking if he survived this mission, then life was a downhill coast from now on.

He made it as far as the tree line bordering the paddy, then was forced to release his hold on Broderick, letting him slip to the ground. Mullins leaned against a tree and drank from his nearly empty canteen. He was at that point of exhaustion where he didn't care if he lived or not. Suddenly, Lofton showed up.

"Jeffrey radioed. Said the Bright Light has been delayed. ARVN unit in trouble. Let's get Austin over to the crater."

"Fuck."

Mullins frowned. Not only was he was deeply concerned about the fate of their team leader, wondering if he'd shaken off the NVA, but now he worried about their own dire situation. He knew it would be some time before another Bright Light team could reach them.

Mullins lifted Broderick, draping him over his shoulder like a sack of feed grain and followed Lofton toward the crater.

When they reached the crater, Mullins eased Broderick into the shell crater and propped him up against the blackened earth. Broderick was still unconscious and Mullins joined Lofton at the base of the crater.

"Good God, Almighty," Lofton uttered. Despite the heat, he felt a chill pass over him. "Look at that."

Mullins' gaze followed Lofton's. He felt his stomach churn. From the tree line at the north end of the rice paddy, scores of NVA soldiers approached, AKs with fixed bayonets trained on their position. Without a word, they began pulling grenades and magazines of ammo from their web gear and laying them out on the rim of the crater.

"God help us," Lofton said under his breath.

* * *

Tran barked orders to his men. They quickly gathered two long, stout branches and laid them a meter apart next to the American. They wrapped the enemy's U.S. Army poncho across the poles, creating a makeshift stretcher, and rolled the American onto it. It took two soldiers at either end to lift him. The American groaned. Tran instructed the bearers to hurry and they quickly carried him into the woods. He and Nguyen held back several meters, fearing the other Americans would return to search for their comrade.

They followed a combination of animal tracks and an obscure network of trails created by the villagers during years of hunting in the jungle forest. It took them less than twenty minutes to reach the underground bunker. They descended the dank, dark tunnel entrance until they came to a broad, earthen room. Rows of wood and canvas cots lined both sides of the room. A few soldiers occupied the cots and they dumped the American onto an empty one.

Tran summoned an orderly and instructed him to undress the American and clean his wounds. He left the ward and entered an adjoining room. A soldier with a cut on his forearm sat on a stainless steel operating table in the middle of the room. Tran stood beside a steel-and-glass case filled with surgical instruments, while he waited for Major Zinh, the battalion doctor, to dress the soldier's arm. When the doctor was done, Tran went over to him.

"Sir, we have captured an American," Tran said without a trace of emotion. "He is wounded and has lost blood. Battalion headquarters will want him alive for interrogation."

Zinh, short and portly, waddled across the room to a washbasin and scrubbed his blood-stained hands with disinfectant. He grabbed a towel from a drawer in another case, wiped his hands dry, and without a word walked out into the ward. Tran shrugged and followed him.

The orderly had stripped the fatigue shirt off the American and turned him over onto his stomach. He cleansed the wound in his lower shoulder with a sponge. Zinh bent over the prisoner, and prodded the flap of purplish flesh with his pudgy fingers. The American cried out when the doctor spread the wound open with his thumb and index finger, and peeled back the puffy skin.

"Turn him over," the doctor ordered. The orderly flipped him on his back. The exit point of the wound, just above his right pectoral, was three times larger than the entry wound. Zinh pressed his obese face close to the American's chest and peered inside. Blood oozed from the wound. Zinh grabbed the sponge from the orderly and jammed it inside the hole, twisting it with deliberate slowness. The American writhed and cried out. Tran and the orderly held him still. Satisfied with his examination, Zinh stood and tossed the sponge onto the American's chest.

"Finish cleaning him," he said to the orderly, "then bring him into the operating room."

- CHAPTER FIVE -

LATE AFTERNOON SUN BURST from behind the airfield control tower with the intensity of an atomic blast, casting a fierce, harsh light on the concrete tarmac. McShane hesitated for a moment in the open doorway of the Operations Center before he stepped out onto the sidewalk. Squinting, he studied the heat waves, shimmering above the runway. The day seemed brighter than usual, likely due to the vast quantity of beer he had consumed the night before. But he didn't want to consider that. It was just another bright, hot South Vietnam day, he convinced himself.

The pilots' briefing was the standard: location of primary and alternate LZs, estimated number of enemy forces in the AO, actions taken if they encountered hostile fire during insertion, wind speed and direction, airspeed, ETA to target. And on and on.

McShane immediately began perspiring as he crossed the expanse of gray concrete to the helipad four hundred meters east of the Dak To airfield. Dark patches of sweat formed beneath his arms. He shielded his eyes against the blaze of light, cursing himself for forgetting his sunglasses. But there wasn't time to remember everything. Owens saw to that.

Today was supposed to be his day off. Half of his indigenous team was on a five-day stand down, having just completed a mission the day before, and were scattered all over Kontum province. Luon, his interpreter, and Trieu, his M-79 man, had stayed behind. The night before he had promised himself he would sleep until noon. Unfortunately, he hadn't informed Owens, the FOB's operation sergeant.

A little after 0800, a furious pounding awakened him from a sound sleep. Groggy and hungover, he initially thought the pounding was in his head, a result of countless cans of Black Label consumed the night before. When the thumping grew louder and more rapid, he realized the awful racket came from the team room door. He staggered over to the door and unlatched it. Owens stepped in.

"Get your shit," he'd commanded. "Slade's in trouble. You're going in with RT Oregon on a Bright Light. Get whoever is available from your team. Chopper's leaving for Dak To in thirty minutes.

That was six hours ago. It was a typical hurry up and wait scenario. They had been stuck on the tarmac at Dak To airfield awaiting aircraft since 0900. The two UH-1B slicks and two AH-1G Cobra gunships to be used for their Bright Light operation had abruptly been re-assigned and sent on another operation in support of an ARVN unit. The choppers had only arrived back from that mission a half-hour ago. They were now refueling and replacing their armaments. This so called "Vietnamization" was killing them. When had helping an ARVN unit become more important than rescuing a SOG team, he wondered. McShane feared their Bright Light team would be inserted too late to be any help.

The Bright Light had originally consisted of two teams, Oregon and Alabama, and had been on alert since the previous afternoon. However, Alabama was sent on another Bright Light operation before they knew of the trouble with Slade's team. At the last moment, Owens decided to substitute his team, RT Illinois, as the Bright Light team. Once McShane learned it was Kevin Slade's team in trouble, he'd readily accepted.

From the day they'd sat next to one another on a flight from San Francisco to Than Son Nhut, he and Slade had been friends. They were both beginning their third tour. Amazingly, their paths had never crossed. Slade had spent his previous tours in the southern part of the country, in the Delta, and McShane had always been in the north, in the Central Highlands. In between jaunts to Vietnam, Slade was assigned to 10th Group in Germany, and for a time languished in purgatory in 3rd Group at Bragg. Both had trained as weapon's specialists, although a year apart. Slade had only recently been reassigned to Kontum from down south. They both had a fondness for beer, which they cultivated on every possible occasion.

The indigenous team members from RT Oregon squatted in the shade of the two slicks. The gunships, armed with rockets and General Electric four-thousand-round-a-minute Gatlin guns, were parked nearby. Brad Erickson, McShane's One-One, was stretched out fast asleep beneath the gunship. He'd celebrated their successful five-day mission with McShane the night before. Even though they were due a five-day stand down, he had eagerly volunteered to join the Bright Light. McShane crouched down and nudged him in the side.

"We're going in," McShane informed him. "I just hope it's not too late. It'll be too dark to fly in another couple hours or so. We might have to spend the night. Get Wolf and Barnett to get their team on the choppers."

Erickson opened one eye at a time and, without a word, crawled from under the Cobra. Rubbing his eyes with the palms of his hands, he walked over to Wolf. David Wolf was RT Oregon's One-Zero and a close friend of Slade's. He crouched against a tree stump, left over from when the wood line surrounding the airfield was cleared ten years before. His eyes were closed when Erickson approached.

"I know, I heard," Wolf said. He sighed, opened his eyes and stood slowly. He grabbed his rucksack, normally bulging with a five-day supply of rations, extra batteries for the radio, a couple pairs of clean socks, and extra ammo for his CAR-15, was now filled primarily with ammo and grenades. He'd only brought along two rations, not expecting to spend much time on the ground.

Wolf found Charlie Barnett sitting in the shade of the slick with Wayne Croft, who chatted animatedly with two members of their four-man Montagnard team. Barnett was Oregon's One-One and radio operator, and had gone through Special Forces Training Group with Slade. Also volunteering for the mission was Croft, a FOB medic, and the only American at the FOB who had bothered to learn the Rhade' hill tribe language.

"Time to get the show on the road, gentlemen," Wolf said.

Without a word, Barnett motioned the Montagnards toward the first chopper. Barnett and Wolf followed their indig to the Huey. As the indig team member boarded, Wolf checked each man's M-16 to make sure the selector switch was on safe.

McShane, Erickson, Croft, Luon, and Trieu boarded the other chopper.

At 1640, the slicks and gunships headed east toward Laos. McShane sat cross-legged on the floor next to Barnett. McShane's thoughts were now filled with dread. Such a late start wasn't good. In addition, he was bothered by the fact that they lacked the element of surprise. They were dealing with an enemy who had grown wise over the years. The NVA knew a rescue operation was imminent and would anticipate, even relish their arrival. McShane suspected NVA forces guarded every likely LZ within a five kilometer grid square. Regardless of the risks, however, there wasn't a man at the FOB who wouldn't risk his own life to help out a FOB team member.

When they entered Laotian airspace, the choppers descended rapidly to the treetops. McShane felt the underbelly of their Huey scrape against triple canopy foliage as they skimmed over the monotonous expanse of green jungle. They continued at tree height until they neared Slade's AO, thirty kilometers from the border. There, the Bright Light force would split. Wolf's chopper would make a false insertion to the north of their intended LZ, and his would pretend to insert to the south. The tactic was designed to draw the enemy away from the primary LZ. It worked, sometimes. More often than not lately, they got the shit shot out of them.

McShane's pilot dropped their craft into a postage stamp-size clearing. McShane grabbed a tie down ring on the floor and braced himself. His stomach seemed to rotate a full 360 degrees with the abrupt maneuver, and an acrid wad of the beef hash ration he'd eaten at noon slithered up his throat. Gagging it back, he glanced out the open doorway. The jungle foliage was a blurred collage of greens and browns as it rushed past. They seemed to descend forever, and for a moment he thought the chopper might be out of control and on a collision course.

His fears vanished when the Huey shuddered and their descent slowed. He glanced out the door. They hovered just a few feet off a grassy clearing. The door gunner swung his M-60 machine gun back and forth, searching the tree line for a target. McShane took in the unfamiliar jungle vegetation swirling about them as the pilot rapidly turned the chopper full circle. The pilot brought the Huey out of the hover and throttled upward. Moments later they rejoined Wolf's helicopter and the gunships, and flew low to the south.

The Cobra gunships arrived at the primary LZ a couple of minutes before the slicks. They slowly circumnavigated the area, hoping to draw enemy fire. While the trick was old, sometimes a trigger-happy soldier opened fire, giving away his and his fellows' position. From their aerial reconnaissance, the LZ appeared clear. They radioed ahead to the slick commanders that the LZ was a go.

McShane monitored the pilots' conversations through his headset. When he heard the LZ was clear, he gave Luon and Trieu a thumbs up and a broad smile. The mercenaries grinned back like mischievous children. They loved the cross-border operations more than life itself. Killing communists was their life.

Turning to Erickson, who had dozed through it all, McShane shouted above the whine of the turbine engine, "LZ checks out okay! We'll go in first and set up a defensive perimeter. Wolf will follow."

Erickson and Croft nodded then edged closer to the open doorway on the right side of the Huey. Erickson leaned out the doorway and rested his feet on the skids. Luon and Trieu moved to the left door and sat. Their legs, too short to reach the skids, dangled them over the sides. McShane sat next to them and scanned the jungle.

The slick angled sharply toward the LZ and made a steep ascent. Hovering a couple meters off a mucky brown stream, the team members, one by one, leaped into the ankle high water and dashed into the nearby tree line. The Huey was already ascending by the time the team reached the trees. McShane, Erickson and Croft hunkered down behind a downed silk cotton tree and together scanned the paddy. Luon and Trieu took cover behind a cluster of thin saplings.

The jungle was deathly silent and still. McShane studied the landscape hard for a few minutes then leaned toward Erickson and Croft: "You guys see anything?"

They both shook their head. McShane glanced over his shoulder and caught Luon's attention. He pointed to his eyes then to the jungle. Luon shook his head, too.

McShane unfastened the radio handset from his web gear harness and radioed Wolf's chopper, informing the pilot the LZ was all clear. Within a couple minutes the slick with Wolf's team bore down on the LZ. It settled into a hover a few meters from their position, and within moments Wolf's team was on the ground and sprinting toward the trees.

The choppers would remain in the general vicinity for upwards of thirty minutes, at which time they'd swoop in to retrieve the teams if they were successful in rescuing Slade's men. After that, they were on their own until the choppers refueled.

Wolf's team joined McShane's and took up defensive positions behind trees and logs. Wolf crouched down next to McShane and together they observed the surrounding jungle for signs of life. McShane noted the sun was already settling behind the mountains. It would be dark soon. If they didn't locate Lofton by the time the choppers returned to refuel, the teams would be forced to remain overnight.

McShane was surprised at the absence of enemy activity. He'd have bet all the beer in Vietnam they would have encountered NVA resistance by now. But then, perhaps they were waiting for the opportunity to launch an all out assault? What was of even greater concern was the lack of radio contact with Lofton. The last communication picked up by the FAC pilot, Captain Jeffrey, who'd continuously monitored

Lofton's radio transmissions, stated they had one WIA and two MIA and were en route to the paddies. But then that was over six hours ago. Anything could have happened since then.

McShane turned to Erickson, who'd been trying to raise Lofton on the radio ever since their arrival. "Still nothing, huh?" Erickson shook his head.

"David, it's not looking good." McShane began, speaking to Wolf who was crouched next to him. "We should have heard from Lofton by now. The choppers will be going back soon and it's getting dark. I'm going to take my team around the trees to the other side of the paddies. Your team will provide security. I'll call if I need help."

McShane's team struck off through the jungle, remaining just inside the vegetation as they circled around the paddies. Besides keeping an eye out for Lofton, he also searched for a suitable RON site. It was unlikely they were going to make it out by nightfall if Lofton didn't show up in the next fifteen minutes or so.

They reached the opposite side of the rice paddies in five minutes. He told Luon and Trieu to move into the jungle to look for Slade's team, but to be gone no longer than ten minutes.

As they disappeared into the dense undergrowth, McShane and Erickson walked along a paddy dike that paralleled the tree line. McShane eyed a shell crater a dozen meters or so away, but it didn't show signs it may have been used by the team for cover.

Off in the distance, McShane heard two, dull, barely audible explosions, followed moments later by two more. They sounded like 2.75 inch gunship rockets. He suspected the Cobras had found a target of opportunity. His attention was abruptly diverted to a sudden movement behind a hedgerow. Erickson heard it, too, and they both turned toward the sound, weapons poised.

They approached the hedgerow wearily: McShane coming in at a crouch from the left and Erickson from the right. Less than a meter from where they saw the movement, a man, his face bloodied, stood up and grinned.

Even through all the blood, McShane recognized him instantly. It was Slade's interpreter, Lap. As he stepped forward, McShane also noticed the left sleeve of his fatigue shirt was torn and his arm was covered with dried blood. Tears came to his eyes when he approached the two Americans.

"Where's Slade and the team?" McShane asked Lap.

"Soldiers shoot Lofton, Broderick, and Mullins. Soldiers take Slade. Maybe dead. Not know. Soldier shoot me in arm. I escape, and hide in woods. Wait for you."

McShane was stunned. Never had he suspected the mission would end this way. Three Americans dead, and one possibly captured. He dreaded what unspeakable horrors could befall Slade at the hands of some sadistic NVA soldier.

Well, there was no way they could call for an extraction now. They'd RON for the night and at first light conduct a search for bodies. There was still a chance that they might find Slade.

* * *

McShane was up before dawn. He'd only grabbed snatches of sleep. Images of mutilated bodies had filled his dreams. While he wasn't a religious man, he prayed to God Slade had either escaped and was hiding in the jungle, or had been killed outright. The NVA so hated SOG teams they often tortured team members mercilessly. On more than one occasion, he'd witnessed first-hand what the NVA were capable of doing to a human body. He'd once seen a man who'd been eviscerated and then his exposed intestines set on fire with a flame thrower. He'd thrown up on the spot.

He had little desire to eat, but choked down a few bites of a chili con carne freeze-dried ration, mixed with tepid water from his canteen. He knew he'd need energy before they headed out. The team's first stop would be the village of Muong May, Slade's original destination. While he didn't count on it, the village might offer clues as to what happened to the team.

After a thorough search of the jungle around the rice paddies, both teams regrouped and McShane led them through the jungle toward the village. It was eerily quiet and McShane was struck with a sense of foreboding. Why hadn't they encountered any bad guys? Had they been scared off at the thought of a B-52 raid? Well, they had every right to be afraid, because that was exactly what was going to happen once the teams were extracted.

When they neared the western edge of the village, he had the teams form a defensive perimeter in the wood line. Lap's wounds had not been serious, and, once Croft cleaned and bandaged them, he was willing to lead them to the village. Along with Lap, McShane and Wolf moved in to get a closer look.

They found a low hedgerow paralleling a narrow road. At the end of the road they made out several huts. Off to their left was a small rice paddy, just large enough to set down a Huey. If the village was occupied with as many NVA as Slade had reported to Captain Jeffrey, it would be suicidal to attempt an extraction from the paddy.

Using the hedgerow as cover, Lap crouched low, and cautiously led McShane and Wolf toward the huts. Suddenly, McShane tripped. Wolf was nearly abreast of him and caught him before he fell. McShane turned to investigate. He was stunned. Partially hidden in the brush was the body of an NVA soldier. Upon closer inspection, they noticed his neck had been nearly severed.

"Slade kill this soldier." Lap said matter-of-factly, and pointed into the jungle. "Soldier bicycle over there."

Several meters from where they found the body, they discovered the bicycle, its frame badly bent, lying beneath a pile of brush. McShane made a cursory check of the bike, looking for a bag or basket that might contain documents, while Wolf looked in the dead soldier's pockets for useful intelligence. Discovering nothing further, they headed toward the village.

They moved in to within twenty-five meters of the first row of huts. From this vantage point, they saw no evidence of life. They observed the village for a few minutes, searching for signs of human activity. At the far end of the village, tucked into the jungle growth, they noticed a large cage fashioned from bamboo poles lashed together with vines and hemp rope. It was roughly two meters high and three or four meters long, McShane estimated. Large enough, he surmised, to house a dozen or more prisoners.

McShane and Wolf approached the bamboo cage wearily, weapons poised. McShane opened the crudely constructed bamboo door and entered. Wolf remained outside, keeping watch while McShane inspected the interior.

There were several slated bamboo sleeping mats spread out on the bare earth. McShane picked up each one with the tip of his weapon's barrel. He wasn't sure what he was searching for, perhaps evidence an American had been incarcerated in the cage. In the far corner of the cage was a narrow elongated trench that had been dug into the dirt. As McShane approached the hole, he knew immediately what its purpose was. There were piles of feces in the pit, covered with flies and maggots. He couldn't imagine living in such conditions and wondered if Slade and his team had been held here, subjected to unimaginable horrors by their NVA captors.

To date, no American POW had ever been rescued from his North Vietnamese captors. McShane hoped to change that. As he rummaged through the contents of the cage, the only thing he discovered was a clay bowl full of maggots, scrounging the last remnants of a grain of rice.

McShane was both discouraged and saddened they hadn't found any signs of the team. He would call in the grid co-ordinates of the village for a later B-52 Arc Light bombing mission. The bamboo enclosure gave McShane the chills and he hurriedly ushered Wolf back into the village.

For the remainder of morning the teams inspected each of the huts, outbuildings, and surrounding fields and rice paddies. It was a strange feeling to find not a single sign of human life. They walked along the nearby narrow road, investigated the log-and-earthen-bunker complex, even sat at one of the long, wooden tables to rest.

Lap, accompanied by Luon and Trieu, retraced the route he'd taken with Slade, but found nothing. Two of Wolf's indig followed the road to the river and reported back that the bridge had been blown. McShane knew, however, the NVA would have the bridge rebuilt by the end of the week, ready for convoys of trucks transporting fresh supplies and troops.

By noon, McShane decided to call off the search. The NVA had likely buried the bodies, or, if there were survivors, taken them prisoner and moved them to another location. He instructed Erickson to radio Captain Jeffrey for an extraction. The team returned to their drop off point, this time cutting directly across the paddies. An hour later, the slicks returned and picked them up. The first thing he intended to do when they got back to the FOB was have S-3 order that Arc Light.

-CHAPTER SIX-

THE AMERICAN HAD ONLY been out of surgery for an hour when two of Sergeant Tran's soldiers pulled him from the dispensary cot. Since he was still groggy and unable to stand from the anesthetic, the soldiers half carried and half dragged him through the earthen corridor. Smoke from animal fat lamps placed in cutouts along the walls filled the tunnel with a heavy stench. Tran had never grown accustomed to the odor. It was all he could do to keep from retching.

Tran welcomed the smell of the musty jungle air as they exited the tunnel entrance. He breathed deeply, attempting to clear his head. Suddenly, two Cobra gunships passed overhead. Tran hurried to the battered, green Datsun pickup and supervised the loading of the American.

The soldiers climbed into the back, one on either side of their prisoner. Tran slid into the passenger seat next to his driver, Private Ngo. The heat was stifling in the cab. He motioned Ngo to start the engine, and then cranked down the window. It became stuck halfway. Tran swore when the window crank broke off in his hand. It was going to be a long drive he told himself.

"Hurry!" Tran shouted. "The Americans will be here soon." The din from an approaching Huey's rotor blades swelled and receded as it made a low pass over the men in the truck.

Unfamiliar with the truck that had only last week belonged to an International Volunteer Service agricultural teacher whose body now lay rotting in the jungle, Ngo released the clutch too rapidly. The truck lurched forward, slamming Tran's head into the cab's rear window. Tran screeched obscenities at Ngo and warned him to be more careful. If any additional harm came to the prisoner, he informed Ngo, he would find himself walking point with a combat unit in the South. Ngo nodded and maneuvered the Datsun deftly around a series of potholes that pocked the narrow dirt road. He glanced over his shoulder to check on their captive, who appeared unconscious.

Tran gladly accepted the responsibility of transporting the American prisoner to a safer location, a hidden jungle camp sometimes used as a POW processing center. Soon, he knew, the enemy helicopters would bring in a large rescue force. They would be heavily armed, and a clash with the American soldiers would be intense and bloody.

His greatest fear, however, was not the enemy soldiers, but the gunships. He'd seen the destructive power of their rapid-fire-mini-guns often enough. His brother and cousin had been killed in a rocket attack during an American rescue mission. Over the years, he'd lost dozens of friends and comrades. He was weary of the war and hoped it would be over soon.

Since Tet, in 1968, when so many young, brave soldiers were slaughtered, he had thought of defecting to the South. He felt the leadership in the North had lost sight of their goal to reunite the two countries. They had become mired in a military complex that served only to kill and maim and destroy. So many comrades were sacrificed to a cause very few of them understood. Hundreds more were still dying. It was time for peace and reconciliation and rebuilding.

They drove east over a hard-packed road, carved through the triple canopy jungle by hundreds of Laotian work crews. From the air, the road was invisible. Ngo shifted down to second gear as they began their ascent over the mountain slope. The road led into the Kamon Valley and then northeast along the Kamon River to the second battalion headquarters. Like their own camp, the battalion was underground, a necessary precaution since the Americans had stepped up the bombings of their sanctuaries in the late 1960s.

The truck began to fishtail on the rain-slick road. Tran held tightly to the door handle as the cab bucked and heaved over potholes. A seat spring worked its way through the thin fabric and jammed Tran in the ass. He swore and turned to Ngo. Perspiration poured from the private's brow. His eyes were locked on the narrow mud lane.

"Drive more carefully, Private!" Tran shouted above the din of the whining engine.

Ngo frowned. "But Sergeant, the road is full of holes."

"And I'll shoot *you* full of holes if you don't drive more carefully!" Tran yelled.

"Yes, Sergeant Tran." Ngo bit his lip before he said something he'd regret. It wasn't proper to question his superior. What did he know, anyway? He was just a recruit.

Tran felt bad for reacting so harshly. It's the damn heat, he thought. It fueled his irritability. He was fast reaching the point where walking was better than spending another moment in the cramped cab. If only he could open the window.

Even after years of fighting in the South, he had never grown accustomed to the heat. Born and raised on a pig farm in Dong Van, three kilometers south of the China border, he was used to far cooler weather. He closed his eyes and tried to remember the feel of the harsh, chilled wind whipping across iced-over rice paddies during winter months, a wind that froze exposed flesh in minutes, a wind that one year killed half their stock before he and his father could get them to shelter. A wind he would give a year's pay to feel swirl through the cab for a single moment.

When they reached the crest of the grade, Tran told Ngo to pull off to the side into some brush and stop. Tran got out and stretched. A light breeze blowing from the north stirred the dank air. It was a comforting relief. He walked around to the truck bed and bent over the side. The American was conscious and peered at him suspiciously. He wished he could speak English. Perhaps the prisoner understood Vietnamese.

"My name is Sergeant Tran," he said in deliberate, slow Vietnamese. "What is yours?"

The American blinked then gazed up at the sky through a narrow opening in the jungle canopy. He ran his tongue across his dry lips. Tran wondered if he understood his question. He watched curiously as he licked his lips again.

"Private," Tran said to the soldier sitting to the American's right, "give him some water." The soldier held out a large canvas water bag to the prisoner.

The American raised his head slowly. The other soldier reached behind him and supported his back. The prisoner drank slowly. When he was done, he wiped his lips and returned the bag to the soldier. Tran nodded his approval.

"My name is Slade," the prisoner suddenly said in halting Vietnamese. He smiled then said, "I am lost."

The soldiers laughed. What an understatement, Tran thought. Was he delirious from the anesthetic and the heat? Or was he trying to be humorous?

"You were wounded by one of our soldiers. You are now our prisoner."

The American appeared baffled. "Where are you taking me?"

Tran was about to reply, but turned abruptly. Off in the distance, he heard the sounds of helicopters. The Americans would be here soon.

"We must go. Watch him carefully," Tran said harshly to the soldier with the water bag.

Ngo jammed the shift lever into first and popped the clutch again. This time he depressed the accelerator at the precise moment and the truck leaped forward without jerking. They crested the slope and began a long descent into the valley. The truck gathered speed quickly. Suddenly they began to slide from side to side on the mud track. Ngo gripped the vibrating steering wheel. His hands trembled as he downshifted back into first and braked hard, nearly causing the Datsun to spin into the brush.

"Be careful, you idiot!" Tran shouted.

The soldiers guarding the American had their hands full, trying to keep their prisoner and themselves from being thrown out of the truck. Finally, Ngo regained control and the vehicle slowed. The remainder of the downhill trip was uneventful.

As they neared the valley floor, the dense vegetation opened up. They could hear the rushing waters of the Kamon River crashing against granite boulders. A narrow suspension bridge, constructed of teak logs and bamboo, spanned the raging waters. Tran was amazed that the bridge was intact. At least once a month, American helicopters or VNAF warplanes destroyed it. Within days, however, local hill tribe poppy growers would rebuild the bridge. They needed it as much as the NVA to transport the raw opium to Chinese drug traffickers at the border. The opium was smuggled into South Vietnam where it was processed into Heroin.

Ngo approached the bridge cautiously. He had never learned to swim, and was deathly afraid of water.

"Hurry, Ngo! Do you want the Americans to see us?" Tran shouted as he slid his left foot over and pressed down on the accelerator. The truck lurched forward. "Get across before we are blown across!"

The bridge was less than seventy-five meters long. Because of the truck's speed, the bamboo decking began to undulate at mid-span, setting up a swaying motion of the entire structure. Ngo panicked and let up on the gas. The truck came to a halt.

Tran scowled at his driver. He turned and glanced out the rear window. The guards in back looked anxiously at the sky. The prisoner sat up, his lips pulled back in a sly grin. Tran tightened his grip on the AK between his legs.

"Drive for the trees," Tran ordered.

Ngo's eyes bulged in fear. He stepped hard on the pedal and the truck lurched forward. The bridge began rocking again, but he didn't care. He feared the gunships more than anything. He didn't want to be split apart by their rockets and machine guns. Never did he want to live more than now. The crude structure creaked, but he ignored the ominous sound. He kept his gaze fixed straight ahead, trying to ignore the roar of the rapids just a few meters below.

It was too late, Tran realized. They had been spotted. The Cobras bore down on them from the south. Tran began to open the passenger door. He would take his chances in the water rather than be dismembered by rockets.

The lead gunship banked hard to the west, up river, and swooped in low. The second Cobra followed several hundred meters behind. They flew only slightly higher than the bridge. Tran could almost make out the lead pilot's features as they closed on the truck.

Ngo had less than twenty meters before he reached the other side, when the pilot released the first of his 2.75-inch rockets. Tran cringed. He flung open the door and stood on the running board. The pilot's aim was high; the rockets spun harmlessly over the cab. Tran, as well as the soldiers in the back, opened fire on the helicopter as it passed over them. Tran wondered why the pilot didn't use the mini-guns? Perhaps he was toying with them? Well, Tran wasn't going to wait for the second gunship pilot to get them in his sights.

"Jump!" Tran hollered to Ngo just as the pilot released a pair of rockets.

Tran leaped from the truck, unsure whether the others had heard him. Out of the corner of his eye, he thought he saw someone crawl out of the truck bed. He couldn't be certain. A deafening roar filled the jungle as a rocket burst the engine compartment apart, severing the Datsun just forward of the cab. The other rocket impacted just behind the truck, splintering a swath out of the bamboo decking several meters long. The rear half of the truck, along with its occupants, toppled backwards into the swift current.

It seemed he would never hit the water. The two explosions sent a searing wave of heat that spun him around like a child's wooden top. Tran envisioned himself floating through the air while rockets and bullets tore away his charred flesh a centimeter at a time. Finally, mercifully, he was swallowed by the churning white water.

Within moments, he was swept far away from the burning bridge. His body tumbled and twisted out of control. The swirling water sucked him further and further beneath the surface of the chilled river. He was completely disoriented, not knowing up from down, life from death. An immense jolt of pain racked his right shoulder as he slammed into a submerged boulder. He began to panic. This wasn't how he wanted to die. A soldier didn't drown; he died bravely in battle fighting for his cause. Tran began to fight back, clawing and kicking at the churning water, praying that he was pointed in the right direction.

Suddenly, he burst from the raging current, gasping for air. He spun around, trying to get a fix on his position. A black plume of smoke spiraled upward from the bridge. The swift current had already carried him a couple of hundred meters downstream. Tran watched in horror as a pair of rockets slammed into the bridge, toppling it into the river. He began swimming toward the riverbank, a few dozen meters to his right.

Weary from exhaustion, he crawled onto a boulder and collapsed. The hard granite surface was warm, comforting. He remained there shivering, trying to catch his breath, and gazed upstream toward the bridge. When the helicopters returned for another pass, he crawled into the brush. Tran wondered if his men had survived, and what had become of the American. He waited in the brush until the helicopters left, and made his way up the bank to search for survivors.

* * *

The pain was beyond anything Slade had ever experienced. The two soldiers dropped him onto his shoulder in the back of the truck. He drew blood as he bit down hard on his lip to keep from crying out. They threw a canvas tarp that reeked of decaying fish over him. The stench was overwhelming, and he might have thrown up had he not been so conscious of the pain. Mercifully, he passed out.

He was largely unaware of the roller-coaster drive, lapsing in and out of consciousness as they bumped along the twisting mountain road. He remembered coming to once and talking to the Vietnamese sergeant, who gave him some water that tasted like mud. Shortly afterwards he lapsed into unconsciousness again.

Not until he heard the Cobras approach did he awaken. Just as the Datsun's bald tires eased onto the bridge's bamboo decking, he sat up and glanced around. He pushed aside the foul smelling tarp. The two soldiers pointed their AK-47s at the sky. Their eyes bulged in fear as they sighted on the rapidly approaching gunships.

Slade's heart raced. He was both excited and afraid. Could the pilots see him partially hidden under the tarp? He kicked the canvas away from his body. Ignoring the pain, he waved his arms in a frantic attempt to signal the pilots not to fire. The soldiers suddenly opened up on the Cobras, but their fire was ineffective. The AK bullets either missed entirely, or ricocheted off the armor plating.

The soldiers continued firing, unaware that Slade was conscious, now leaning over the down-river side of the truck bed. Slade studied the churning waters. Unless he wanted his body ripped apart by American rockets, the river was his only choice. Keeping a wary eye on the soldiers, he carefully maneuvered to the edge of the truck bed and climbed over the side. The truck abruptly picked up speed, nearly tossing him back onto the tarp, but he clung desperately to the side. He rolled over onto the bamboo decking just as the first rocket spiraled toward the truck.

Slade misjudged the speed of the truck and bounced hard on the bridge's surface. The bamboo was slick and he was unable to maintain his balance. He reached for one of the bridge's woven hemp suspension lines, but it was beyond his grasp. Suddenly, his body was racked by a fierce, thundering explosion. He felt his body elevate as a wave of hot air picked him up and hurled him away from the bridge. The roar from the detonating rocket nearly burst his eardrums, drowning out the sounds around him. The river grew instantly silent. He was momentarily reminded of the quiet during a parachute jump.

It seemed as though he tumbled through the air for a lifetime. At one point, he caught a glimpse of the bridge on fire. His last thought before he plunged into the river was that he wished he had his wetsuit.

The chilled waters closed around him. His arm slammed against a rock. He roared in pain, but it came out only as a gurgle. He swallowed too much water. Panic began to set in. He started to gag as he was swept along the river bottom.

Slade struggled frantically to reach the surface. He knew it was within his reach, but the riptide kept tugging at him, pulling him farther underneath. This is bullshit, he thought to himself. I could out-swim anyone in high school.

He aimed his body toward the surface and began to swim with the current. As he suspected, he was only a few feet below the surface. He came to the top retching. His chest heaved frantically as his lungs sucked in the humid air. The pain in his shoulder was overwhelming, and for an instant, he thought he would pass out. He rolled over onto his back and allowed the current to pull him downstream. He gazed upstream. The bridge was severed and there was no sign of the truck.

Now out of the rapids, he drifted with the current, eyes closed. The pain in his shoulder subsided. For a time, he daydreamed of the Labor Day weekend he'd spent at Cape Hatteras, North Carolina, surfing with a ten-foot surfboard he'd rented from a surf shop beneath a weathered-gray pier, built at the turn of the century by whalers. He'd spent most of that blistering hot morning trying to get the hang of it.

Finally, sunburned and tired, he loaned the fiberglass board to a good looking brunette with emerald eyes who'd watched him flounder in the surf. He could still recall her piercing gaze and her soft southern manner when he offered her the board. When she asked him, in a licorice-sweet North Carolina drawl, to help her carry the board to the beach, he blushed and fell instantly in love.

They frolicked in the gently lapping waves, taking turns with the awkward-sized board for the remainder of the afternoon. Her name was Stephanie, and she worked for a private employment agency in Charlotte. Late in the afternoon, she tired of the board, thanked him and left the beach with a man she said was her husband. He sprawled on the warm sand, head resting on the tip of the board for better than an hour, thinking of all the things they'd do together if he was her husband.

The river narrowed substantially, and Slade floated beneath some low overhanging brush that scraped against his face. Startled, he snapped his eyes open, and righted his body. His feet touched the river bottom and he was able to stand. The water lapped at his chin. The river was no longer in the open, but covered over by a thick canopy of trees and vines. It was dark and strangely quiet. He looked upstream. The bridge, or where it had once stood, was beyond his view. He was shocked at how far he'd drifted.

He waded over to the riverbank and climbed up through the brush until he cleared the rocky embankment, and was on solid ground. The forest was as thick as any he'd ever encountered. He felt safe. He figured if he couldn't see more than a few meters, then he couldn't be seen, either.

He crawled over to a tree and sat against it. The black, pajama pullover top the NVA had dressed him in was ripped across the chest, and he was able to get a clear look at his wound. Slade absorbed what he saw and wanted to scream. A bloated, coal-black leech burrowed between the stitches, methodically chewing at the tender incision. Slade shuddered at the sight and quickly reached in and ripped the loathsome creature away. He closed his fist around the leech and squeezed until the parasite burst.

He was suddenly famished and glanced around, searching for something edible. The forest floor was covered with broad-leafed ferns, ankle-high grasses and rotting deadfall. Unfortunately, he thought, no fast-food drive-ins. He imagined that if he poked among the deadfall he might uncover a lizard or grasshopper or even a wood rat. But without a knife for filleting or matches for a fire, he'd have to gobble them raw. The thought made him nearly puke. You're some bad-ass Green Beret, he told himself.

He now wondered how far away he was from the LZ. Fording the river was his first obstacle. Once on the other side, he'd try to locate the road they'd been traveling, and follow it. With any luck at all, it would take him toward Muong May. The gunships that had fired on them were no doubt part of a Bright Light mission searching for his team. But it was nearly dark, and he'd have to wait until morning to make his way back. He slowly stood, wincing at the pain in his shoulder.

The snap of a twig abruptly interrupted his thoughts. He froze in place and turned slowly toward the sound, thinking wild pig or deer. What he saw astonished him.

Less than a dozen meters away, approaching cautiously, weapons drawn, were several loincloth-clad hill tribesmen. In the center of the group, yanked along the ground by a rope tied around his neck was Sergeant Tran. Blood trickled from his nose and cuts on his face and arms.

Slade wasn't sure how he should react. Should he celebrate, or fear for his life? He decided to play it safe and placed his hands on his head. The men, armed with World War II vintage M-1 carbines and Russian SKS rifles, kept their weapons trained warily on him. One of the tribesmen, carrying an AK-47, emerged from the pack. Slade noticed a faded and threadbare unit patch sewed to the left side of his bright red loin cloth.

As the man approached, Slade instantly recognized the emblem. A slight smile came to his lips. The sight of the blue and yellow Special Forces emblem made him momentarily forget his problems. These, he hoped, were remnants of the Meo tribal forces trained by Special Forces White Star teams in the sixties.

The Meo were disliked and held in low regard by the Laotians and Vietnamese. Special Forces had been successful in capitalizing on the Meo's resentment by training and arming these semi-nomadic hill tribe people to fight against both countries' communist forces. They had originally been led by Colonel Vang Pao and were still active in parts of Laos.

Slade waited patiently for the man to approach. A deep scowl etched his leathery-skinned forehead. Slade felt he might have guessed wrong and that these weren't the SF trained Meo, but opium growers who were pissed off because the bridge had been destroyed. He eyed the short, curved dagger tucked into the man's loin cloth. Were he and the North Vietnamese soldier to be sacrificed to some animist god, he wondered?

His skin crawled at the thought of his heart being cut, still beating, from his chest and passed around for all the tribe to snack on.

The man stood directly before him. His intense, dark eyes bore into Slade. Slade began to sweat involuntarily. Two men approached him. He was afraid they were going to tie him up. Instead, one of them grabbed him by his right arm and positioned him behind the tribesman with the SF patch. The other two fell in behind him. Trussed up like a Thanksgiving Day turkey, Tran was pulled along by two others as they filed silently into the forest.

- CHAPTER SEVEN -

Bangkok, Thailand
May, 1992

IT WAS NEARLY DARK when, without warning, a dozen men brandishing stout bamboo clubs emerged from the crowd of pro-democracy demonstrators and lurched toward the police line in front of the Royal Hotel on Ratchadamnern Street. At the same instant, a barrage of fist-sized concrete chunks collected from a nearby demolition site struck several of the policemen as they fought off the attackers.

Two of the uniformed men, bleeding profusely from head wounds, collapsed onto the hotel's marble steps. The frightened, unarmed police edged up the steps dragging the wounded officers with them. Scores of angry demonstrators pressed forward, taking advantage of the retreating police line.

The clatter of diesel engines suddenly filled the steamy night air, as a column of Thai army trucks crammed with soldiers roared down the street toward the besieged hotel. Unaware of the approaching troops, the noisy demonstrators continued to advance on the police, who were now cornered at the top of the hotel steps.

Automatic gunfire erupted from behind the angry crowd, throwing the mob into disarray. Cries of terror and anger spread quickly through the throng of demonstrators, as bloodied men, women, and children fell to the rubble-strewn street. Those uninjured grabbed the wounded and carried them past the shocked police into the hotel lobby.

In the midst of the confusion, a red Nissan taxi pulled abruptly into a narrow alley behind the Royal Hotel and halted near the rear entrance. The Thai driver glanced nervously in the rearview mirror, as sirens wailed in the distance. Four demonstrators, shouting obscenities and waving bamboo clubs, approached the cab. The agitated driver spun around, and faced his passenger in the back seat.

"You get out here," he said quickly. "Go in back door in hotel." He pointed to a pair of glass doors illuminated by the car's headlights. Four stern-faced soldiers in camouflage fatigues, brandishing M-16 automatic rifles, stood guard outside the door. McShane nodded and hurriedly handed him a 500-baht note for the 300-baht trip from the airport. He grabbed his overnight bag, and headed up the long walkway toward the glass doors.

The soldiers eyed McShane suspiciously as he approached. Dressed in light tan shorts and a striped, Jersey-knit shirt, McShane looked like one of the hundreds of Western tourists who normally roamed the Royal Hotel. One of the soldiers shouted something as he neared. Though he did not understand a word of Thai, he understood the tone and stopped immediately. The soldier came up to him, as the others held their weapons at the ready. McShane gave the soldier his best All-American smile.

"Good evening," McShane said. "Nice night for a demonstration."

Ignoring him, the soldier grabbed McShane's bag from his hand. He hurriedly unzipped it and began rummaging through its contents. McShane eyed him curiously, asking himself, *what's he lookin' for, a fuckin' bomb?* Thailand was governed by an ex-Army general, who, only a month before, had made himself Prime Minister. Even so, the behavior of the troops surprised him. They were supposed to protect the hotel guests from the rioters, not intimidate them.

When the soldier failed to find anything subversive, he handed the bag back to McShane, and pointed him toward the door. McShane stuffed a pair of white boxer shorts the soldier had thrown to the walkway during the search back inside the bag and zipped it up.

Stepping through the door, he turned toward the soldier, "Can you tell me where the bar is?"

The soldier frowned and nudged him on through the door with the butt of his weapon. McShane winked back at him and walked briskly up the hall, appreciating the blast of chilled, air-conditioned air.

As he neared the lobby, McShane heard the shrill, tormented screams of people in pain. He was unprepared for the carnage that greeted him when he entered the large, high-ceilinged lobby.

Sprawled across the room's gray-and-black marble floor were dozens of wounded Thai civilians. McShane noted that most appeared to be suffering from gunshot wounds. The floor was awash in blood. A boy, no older than ten, screamed as blood pumped rhythmically from a jagged wound running the length of his lower leg. McShane figured that a round from an M-16 must have struck him in the knee and then tumbled end-over-end along the femur until it exited at the ankle.

McShane knelt beside a nurse, who was desperately trying to tie a tourniquet around the squirming boy's thigh. He reached out and held the child steady then grabbed the kid's leg and put thumb pressure on the artery, allowing the nurse time to tie off the tourniquet. The spurting blood slowed to a trickle and then stopped.

"You'll be okay, son," McShane whispered in the boy's ear.

The child's terror-filled, brown eyes gazed into McShane's and his sobbing eased a bit. McShane felt a soft, light touch on his forearm. He looked up. The young Thai nurse, her light blue uniform splattered with blood, was smiling at him.

"Thank you, sir," she said in halting English.

McShane nodded, thankful to be of assistance. He rose slowly and surveyed the scene. Memories he'd buried long ago suddenly surfaced, and played before him like a news broadcast. He gazed over the writhing bodies in disbelief. How could this happen in a city at peace?

Thailand was one of the wealthiest, most stable countries in Southeast Asia. Tourists flocked by the thousands to chase bargains and deserted white sand beaches. Foreign investment poured in from Japan,

Germany, Australia, and the U.S. What he witnessed was beyond reason, beyond comprehension.

He swallowed hard and made his way carefully across the blood-slick floor. Except for four massive, crystal chandeliers hanging from the center of the lobby there was little evidence of the hotel's opulence. The burgundy, velvet wing-chairs and love seats, hastily pushed to the walls to make room on the floor for the seriously wounded, were filled with injured civilians. Those left standing leaned against the gilded handrail of the curved marble staircase leading to the Olympic-size pool. McShane could only imagine the splendor of the Royal Hotel. Built after World War II, the hotel catered to wealthy Thais and had been the talk of the Pacific Rim. He wished he could have seen it under different circumstances.

White-smocked attendants arrived and wheeled away the more seriously wounded on gurneys to ambulances lined up at the rear entrance. A portly Thai, white sleeves rolled to his elbows, attended to a woman on the polished-teak check-in counter. He covered a length of twisted, small intestines piled on her abdomen with a damp towel. Judging by his precise actions, McShane guessed he was a doctor.

McShane wasn't certain what his next move should be. He was supposed to rendezvous with the team's contact in the hotel bar at eight. However, the bar was now a triage center with nurses and ambulance attendants hastily passing among the wounded.

McShane glanced around the room. He knew what his contact looked like from pictures studied during isolation. All he could focus on, however, were broken bodies lying end to end, and the blood. It seemed everywhere. He turned from the carnage and walked toward the curved staircase. He noticed a plywood sign painted with the word POOL and an arrow pointed upward.

As he climbed the stairs, a Thai in blue jeans and a white T-shirt with "Edmonton, Canada", emblazoned across the front approached. The man wore thick-lensed, wire-framed glasses, and appeared to be in his late forties. McShane nodded and began taking the steps two at a time.

"Great time of year for a ski trip," the man said as he passed him.

McShane stopped instantly. He spun around and replied, "Only if you know how to swim."

"But it is not necessary if you use your poles."

"I think I'll get my hat and meet you in Venice."

The team loved creating these nonsensical code phrases. This was as ridiculous as they got. There was no doubt the man grinning up at him from the bottom of the stairs was his contact.

McShane stepped down and extended his hand. "Mr. Chan, I didn't think I'd find you." Chan clasped his hand and shook it vigorously.

"Mr. McShane, please to meet acquaintance. Sorry, we have little problem. Clear up in couple days."

"A little problem? There are wounded people everywhere. What the hell happened?"

Chan rubbed his brow. "Come, let's go to pool. Quiet there. Can talk much better."

McShane followed the slightly built man up the stairs, through a glass door, and out onto the concrete patio surrounding a kidney-shaped pool. McShane noticed several Westerners, hotel guests probably, sitting in clusters by the pool, talking quietly amongst themselves. Their faces were full of concern.

Chan found a deserted table with two chairs at the far corner of the patio away from the others. He slid a chair out for McShane and waited for him to sit before he did.

"You are right. This is not little problem. This is bad," Chan admitted, shaking his head slowly from side to side. "I will explain. The people angry with government, because Suchinda is Prime Minister. Not elected by people. He is ex-general and picked many army friends to work with him. People tired of army in government. Want Suchinda out. That is why demonstrate. Army responsible for killing. Very bad. Very bad." Chan gazed out across the twinkling lights of the congested city and sighed.

A burst of gunfire from the street below forced their attention downward. "You see," Chan continued, "army continues to fire on own people. Killing only end when Suchinda resigns. Only then will Thai people be satisfied."

McShane felt deep sympathy for Chan and his countrymen, but he couldn't concern himself with the politics of Thailand. He had a mission to carry out and he needed Chan's help.

"Mr. Chan, I am very sorry for what is happening in your country, but I must talk to you about the man you saw on your trekking trip last month, the man in the picture you turned over to our intelligence personnel. He is extremely important to us. We need you to lead us into the mountains where you saw him. Can you do that for us?"

Chan seemed dazed. McShane wasn't sure he'd heard a word. "My instructions," he continued, "are to meet you with five of my men in Chiang Mai, day after tomorrow. Our cover story is that we are American tourists on a trekking trip, visiting the hill tribes and that you are our guide."

McShane avoided revealing all the details of the operation. He didn't want to alert Chan to the possible dangers of the trip. All Chan needed to know was that they were going in to look for an American deserter. He didn't need to know that the other half of the team, or the "B" team, was to be quartered at 1st Special Forces Group "B" Company's headquarters in Lop Buri, 90 miles north of Bangkok.

In the event his "A" team came under fire from Burmese Army troops, they would be standing by, along with two platoons of Royal Thai Rangers and Royal Thai Army gunships, as security for the exfiltration phase of the operation. Chan did not yet know that each of his men would be armed with CAR-15s, four hundred rounds of ammunition, and a half-dozen grenades. Chan would be told the "deserter" was dangerous and that the weapons were for self-defense. McShane, of course, hoped they wouldn't need them. He didn't relish the thought of engaging Burmese forces in a firefight when he was so close to retiring.

"The man you look for," Chan abruptly began, "lives with Karen tribe on Burma side of border. The Karen want separate state for their people. Burma not give them own land. All Karen tribes in Burma unite to fight for own land. But very poor. Not know much about fighting. This man I know teach them how to use weapon, how to fight Burmese soldier. He very proud man. Hate communist. Before he come to Thailand, he help Khmer tribes fight communist Khmer Rouge in Cambodia. Before that he help Meo in Laos fight government. Before that, he prisoner of North Vietnamese in Laos, but he escape. I know tribe where he lives. Yes, I take you there."

What Chan told him was something of a revelation. If the man in the picture proved to be Slade, then a few more pieces of his puzzling past were filled in. Slade's hatred of communism was common knowledge: he witnessed their brutality on many occasions in Vietnam. He had despised the North Vietnamese and, in particular, the Viet Cong, South Vietnam's communist army, for their terror tactics against the Vietnamese people. They looted, raped, taxed, and murdered the village peasants if they didn't cooperate.

The Vietnamese communists often recruited from the same province. These butchers had turned Slade against the "People's Revolutionary Army" during his first tour. Apparently his loathing of communism was as strong as ever. McShane wasn't convinced, however, that was the only reason Slade had remained in Southeast Asia for two decades.

"Good," McShane said. "I will meet you at your office in Chiang Mai Tuesday morning. Do you have any questions?"

"How you get to Chiang Mai?"

"We arranged transportation through a private travel agent in Lop Buri." Yeah, McShane mused, Uncle Sam's Worldwide Travel Agency.

Chan opened his mouth to say something, but closed it quickly and grinned instead. It wasn't his concern how they got there. He had worked for the C.I.A. before and knew not to ask questions. He didn't really believe this man calling himself McShane was after an Army deserter. There had been many articles in the Bangkok Post lately about sightings of Americans near the Thai, Burmese and Lao border. He believed the man McShane was looking for was a Vietnam MIA.

But then that was none of his business, either. His job was to lead them to the border, possibly even into Burma.

As the two men rose from their chairs, their attention was suddenly diverted by the chatter of M-60 machine gun fire from the street below. They crossed the patio and peered over the guardrail at the smoke-filled street. Lifeless forms lay everywhere. The sight was too painful for Chan; he quickly turned away.

"I must go."

"Can I help in any way?" McShane asked, his voice full of concern.

Chan shook his head and walked back into the besieged hotel. McShane stood outside for a time, listening to the sounds of sirens and sporadic gunfire.

After a time, he went into the hotel, deciding that if nothing else, he could mop up some blood.

-CHAPTER EIGHT-

MCSHANE AND THE TEAM left the European Guest House shortly before nine after a breakfast of banana pancakes and coffee. The guesthouse, popular among young European travelers, was owned by Surin, a former Thai Special Forces sergeant, and Patty, his British wife. During the late '60s and early '70s, Surin had rented rooms to CIA operatives and U.S. Special Forces men on R&R from Vietnam. He was still held in high regard by the U.S. government, and was occasionally called on to discretely provide rooms for certain types of government employees.

They climbed into a pair of two-cycle powered, three-wheeled cabs, called tuk-tuks by the locals because of the odd clattering sound the engines made. They were to meet Chan in his office at nine.

As they careened through Chiang Mai's narrow, claustrophobic streets, sometimes on only two wheels, McShane was pleasantly surprised by what he saw. Vastly smaller than Bangkok, Chiang Mai, the country's second largest city, was much less congested. Vehicular and foot traffic moved about the streets relatively freely; this was impossible in Bangkok, which had traffic jams at every intersection. The air was cooler, less humid than the south, and, after two intolerably muggy days, the change was a welcome relief.

With a company of Thai Army Rangers, they had flown aboard a Royal Thai Air Force C-130 to Chaing

Mai the previous night. The rangers were headed for the Burmese border to bolster defensive positions near the town of Naisoi. For the past week, Burmese Army units had been infiltrating across the Thai border in search of Karen guerrillas. Two Thai soldiers had been killed, and a dozen wounded, during Burmese forays into Thailand.

Akaradetch Klinpraneet, the general in command of the Thai border forces, planned a counteroffensive to drive the Burmese back into their country. His orders were to inflict as many casualties as possible to warn the Burmese to stay out of Thailand.

McShane sat directly behind the tuk-tuk driver. Lieutenant Hansen sat next to McShane and the team's intelligence expert, Sergeant Wade Everett, sat next to him. They were fortunate to have Everett on their team. The thirty-six year old sergeant had spent two years on an "A" team in Lop Buri as an assistant intelligence sergeant. His team had made frequent incursions into Laos to search for POWs and MIAs in 1979. On two occasions, they had infiltrated Burma to follow leads from opium growers and drug traffickers with whom Caucasians had been seen working in the opium fields. The men, the team learned, were French and German mercenaries, hired by the drug lord Khun Sa to oversee his opium cultivation operation.

Towards the end of his tour, Everett's team had been part of a Drug Enforcement Agency opium eradication project. He spent three weeks with two DEA agents and a Thai Special Forces team patrolling the hills north of Chiang Mai in search of opium fields.

He spoke Thai with some fluency, was familiar with the mountainous terrain, knew his way around the streets and back alleys of Chaing Mai, and, more importantly, knew the best places to eat and drink Singha, the local Thai beer.

The other tuk-tuk pulled up alongside them. Colin Evans, the team's weapons specialist, leaned over the edge of the railing and shouted above the annoying din of the two-cycle engines.

"Hey, Everett, where're the babes?"

Everett shook his head in disbelief and grinned. "All in good time, Colin. All in good time."

Evans slumped back in his seat. At twenty-three, he was the youngest and the newest member on the team. Six-four with a muscular, tanned build that rivaled Arnold Schwarzenegger's, Evans was an imposing sight next to the short, frail-appearing Thais. Even though McShane was constantly on him about blond hair over the tops of his ears, he liked and respected Evans a great deal.

His knowledge of weapons was encyclopedic. There wasn't a domestic or foreign arm that the brash kid from Ventura, California, wasn't familiar with. He could hump a ruck, as well as the team's M-60, hour after hour, days on end, without complaint, staying up each night until the intricate weapon was cleaned meticulously, whether it was fired or not.

While the bulky M-60 was out of the question for this particular mission, Evans was responsible for maintaining the team's CARs and instructing the Karen guerrillas on the use of the weapons that "B" Company was air dropping next week.

"Keep it in your pants, Colin," interjected Travis Payne, seated next to Evans. "Didn't you pay attention to the Medical Officer's briefing? Three out of every four prostitutes in Thailand has been exposed to the HIV virus."

"No sweat, Payne. I brought protection."

"Well, just make damn sure it doesn't break or slip off. Being from California, you'd have a hard time explaining how you caught AIDS."

"Fuck off, Doc."

As the team medic, Payne had reason to be concerned about Evan's well-being. It was his responsibility to monitor the team members' health. AIDS was no longer a joking matter, relevant only to San Francisco homosexuals. It was rampant among the Thai working girls. He had enough to do, just reminding the team to take their anti-malaria tablets, drink plenty of fluids, keep their feet dry, and watch for poisonous snakes, without losing sleep over their sexual peccadillos.

When he enlisted in the summer after his freshman year at Cal Poly, in the west coast town of San Luis Obispo, Payne's intention was to "take a break from school", "see the world", "find myself", "discover what I want out of life". That's what he told his friends, who were surprised by his announcement. He doubted those were his true reasons for dropping out, but he knew for certain he wasn't eager to muddle through three more years of college, pretending to know the direction he wanted his mediocre life to take, because at the time, he hadn't a clue.

With no burning desire to become an engineer, or biologist, or teacher, he followed his nineteen-year-old instincts and stopped by the local Army recruitment office. Lured inside by a color poster of a C-130 spewing dozens of helmeted parachutists, beneath a brilliant full moon, he decided it looked more appealing than listening to a Psych 101 lecture. In less than an hour he signed up for the U.S. Army Airborne School at Ft. Benning, Georgia and in a week he was flying to Leesville, Louisiana to attend basic training at Ft. Polk. Ten weeks later, he was transferred to Ft. Sam Houston in Texas for combat medic school, and by the time the fall semester commenced, he was in Georgia reporting to jump school.

In three grueling weeks, under an unrelenting Georgia sun, he was transformed into one of the "devils from above" portrayed in the recruiting poster. Another poster on the door of the company re-enlistment office caused him to extend his tour an additional three years. His new vision was to wear a green beret, like the tall, lean soldier repelling down a shear granite cliff depicted in the picture. That had been fourteen years before, ten of those years spent as a medic on this detachment.

Occasionally, he wondered if his friends had found the careers and wealth they were so preoccupied with during their senior year in high school. Were they married, did they have kids, had they grown fat, lost their hair, divorced? While he'd lost some hair, it didn't matter; the Army required it short, anyway. He had never found time to marry. At an even six-feet, he still weighed the same as the day he stepped on the scales at the recruiters: one-eighty. He didn't regret for a minute the abrupt, impulsive career move he had chosen a decade and a half ago.

The team's tuk-tuks stopped in front of the Singha Travel office. Chan was handing cardboard boxes to a puffy-faced, heavy-set Thai standing in the back of a covered Nissan pickup truck. While the team unloaded their rucksacks, McShane gave each of the tuk-tuk drivers a 100-baht note. They nodded approval and roared off in search of another fare. The team carried their rucks to the truck and tossed them in back.

"Good morning, Mr. McShane," Chan said, grinning so widely that McShane thought his cheeks would split.

McShane extended his hand. "Good morning." Chan shook it vigorously.

Poking her head out the office door, Chan's secretary, Sai, interrupted them and told him there was a telephone call.

"Excuse, Mr. McShane." Chan quickly scampered through the door.

McShane stepped into the back of the Nissan, and sat at the end of the bench-seat next to the tailgate. He deeply breathed in the humid morning air. It smelled like garlic and garbage, from food stalls in the open air market next to the travel agency. Charlie Pike, the team's demolitions sergeant, sat down next to McShane, and wrinkled his nose.

"Goddamn, Sarge. That place reeks big time." He pinched his nostrils with thumb and forefinger and turned his head away from the stench. "Do you think we'll be movin' out soon?"

"As soon as Chan gets off the phone," McShane replied.

Pike slid off the seat and onto the pavement. "Sooner the better. I'm going across the street to get a Coke before I puke."

McShane chuckled. He understood how Pike felt. The smell was getting to him, too. "Hey," he called after him. "Get me a Sprite or 7-Up."

Charlie Pike had come to the team directly from Training Group three years before. Compared to others on the team, he wasn't very tall. He stood at just over five-eight, and weighed a solid hundred seventy pounds. But the red-headed, freckled faced kid from Grants Pass, Oregon, was enthusiastic. He was cocky and full of piss and vinegar, ready to take on every low-intensity conflict in the world.

A month after joining the team, he got his first chance, when the team was assigned to El Salvador for a three-month MTT tour. As the junior engineer, he helped the senior demo sergeant, SFC Rodney Poole, with demolitions training for a battalion of Salvadorian infantrymen. Each week, for about a 40-hour work week, they ran a platoon from the unit through their basic course. Class instruction included the use, handling, and detonation of Claymore anti-personnel mines, making up simple charges with C-4 plastic explosive for bridge and rail destruction, conducting demolition reconnaissance, and carrying out a demolition mission.

The Salvadorians were awed by Pike's ability to use the putty-like explosive to fell trees as big around as a tractor tire, to sever steel I-beams as thick as a man's thigh, and to crumble reinforced concrete bridges like they were made of clay. His classes were popular and enthusiastically attended by the young soldiers.

Based on the letters of commendation praising his "excellent achievements and expert handling of troops" in El Salvador, McShane had decided Pike would accompany the team into the mountains of northern Thailand. Besides the M-16s, the "B" Company airdrop included a hundred pounds of C-4, scores of blasting caps, several hundred yards of det-cord, and an M-122 kit that included a transmitter capable of detonating a charge from two miles away. McShane figured Pike's training skills would prove invaluable, training the Karen in the artful use of military explosives.

Still grinning when he came back out to the truck, Chan tossed a small rucksack, with a pair of canvas and rubber boots tied to its side, into the back. He seemed eager to get moving, and motioned to the large, round-faced Thai he called Happy Buddha, to get in the truck.

"We go now. Have maybe five hour for travel to Pai. Have lunch. Drive maybe one hour to Ban Mae La Na, leave truck then walk two hour to Karen village. Stay night in village." He gazed up toward the bright, hazy sky. "Hot today."

No shit, McShane thought. He'd felt the effects of the heat ever since they arrived in Thailand. North

Carolina humidity was nothing compared to Thailand's steam bath atmosphere. He definitely was not looking forward to humping his heavy rucksack.

Pike helped the young female store clerk place two six-packs of Coke into a plastic shopping bag. She giggled at something he'd said.

"Pike!" McShane shouted. "Get your ass in gear, or you can walk!"

He hurriedly jammed a handful of candy bars into the bag, tossed a wad of 100-baht notes on the counter, and sprinted across the street.

Pike handed the bag to McShane and climbed over the side of the truck just as Happy Buddha began to ease away from the curb.

"You'll be thanking me an hour from now, after you've been inhaling exhaust fumes and sucking up dust," Pike said.

"Yeah, yeah. You weren't thinking about us. You were thinking about what's between your legs . . . and the girl's legs." McShane grabbed his forearm when Happy Buddha suddenly slammed on the brakes to avoid a tuk-tuk. "Now sit down before you break your neck."

Happy Buddha shouted something in Thai to the tuk-tuk driver then stomped his size-twelve foot on the throttle. The truck lunged forward, nearly clipping the rear of the three-wheeled motor scooter and throwing Pike onto the wood bench seat between McShane and Payne.

"I love the way they drive in Thailand!" Pike shouted over the din of the cracked muffler.

* * *

The drive to Pai was long and tedious, the monotony broken only by an occasional stop to buy bottled water and snacks from roadside vendors. McShane was impressed with the sweet taste of the fried bananas wrapped in banana leaves. He bought a dozen of the bananas from a vendor and tried passing them around to the team. Only Pike took him up on the offer, eating six of them. McShane kept two and passed the others up to Chan and Happy Buddha.

While the others dozed, McShane gazed at breathtaking views of the forested mountains, lush, brilliant green valleys, and terraced rice paddies covering the nearby hills. Now and then he managed a catnap, catching up on some of the sleep he lost when they skipped a day crossing the international dateline. His thoughts, however, were on the mission and, in particular, Slade. It had been quite a shock after believing for twenty years that he'd died in Laos, suddenly learning he might be alive. It was hard to accept. What was even more perplexing was why he had remained in Southeast Asia all these years. He hoped it wouldn't be long before he discovered the answer.

When they arrived in Pai, Happy Buddha stopped at a small café outside of town. Chan slid the rear window aside, and poked his head through the narrow opening. As usual, he was grinning. "Have lunch here."

Lunch consisted of two huge wooden bowls heaped with pork fried rice, and wide, flat noodles, called rhadnay, topped with fresh vegetables. They ate silently, sitting at a long teak table under a tin overhang that protected them from the mid-day sun. Except for Pike, who ordered a Coke, the team drank bottled water. It was all McShane felt like drinking. Cokes were too sweet, and beer would just make him feel more lethargic than he already did.

They stayed at the restaurant for nearly an hour. Evans and Payne managed a brief nap beneath a broad banana tree behind the restaurant. Lieutenant Hansen had stomach cramps and diarrhea, and skipped lunch. The two Imodium tablets Payne gave him for the diarrhea before lunch hadn't helped and he spent the majority of the time in the outhouse, squatting over the porcelain toilet embedded in concrete.

Pike never stopped eating, ordering an additional bowl of rice and noodles when the main course was gone. He continued to wash the food down with Cokes. Unable to watch him consume another can or cram another spoonful of food into his mouth, McShane and Everett walked back to the truck.

"How can he eat so much in this goddamn heat? Or drink so many Cokes?" Everett asked as he wiped his brow with a paper napkin from lunch. "From the day he joined the team, I knew there was something strange about him. He's not fuckin' human. I think he's an alien from another planet; they've run out of food and his mission is to gobble up as much chow as he can. Then one day, hopefully tomorrow, he'll return, be sliced open and everything he's eaten over the years will be duplicated a zillion times by a proton feeding machine and his planet will be saved, over his dead body."

McShane shook his head. "I don't know who's weirder, Wade, you, or Pike. Go find the L.T. and make sure he hasn't fallen in the crapper. I'll wake the sleeping beauties and get the alien."

Just as Everett turned, Lt. Hansen lurched from the ramshackle, bamboo-thatched outhouse. He walked unsteadily toward the truck. His skin was pale and there were chunks of shrimp omelet from breakfast clinging to his I LOVE THAILAND T-shirt.

"L.T., how was breakfast . . . again?" McShane asked, grinning.

Hansen climbed into the back of the truck. "Tasted about as bad the second time as the first." He sprawled out on the seat. "God, I feel awful. Got it coming out both ends. I don't know whether to shit or go blind."

"Drink some water. I don't want you dehydrated. We still have a long walk ahead of us."

Hansen groaned then sat up. He drank slowly from a plastic water bottle he pulled from beneath the seat. "I don't think I can hold it down." He hung his head over the side of the truck and threw up.

"Wade, get the L.T. a couple electrolyte drinks," McShane ordered. "He might have better luck." Everett began to make his way to the little store adjacent to the restaurant. "And tell the others to hurry up," he called out. "I want Doc to check out the L.T."

Chan and Happy Buddha had been sitting with the restaurant owner's wife. When they saw that the team had reassembled inside the truck, they held their hands together as if in prayer, and bowed their heads. Chan thanked the lady for her hospitality. The two hurriedly returned to the truck, and within moments they were back on the two-lane highway.

Hansen had better luck with the green electrolyte drink Everett brought back. He drank half the bottle without adverse reaction. Payne diagnosed food poisoning, probably from the shrimp they'd eaten the night before. He advised Hansen to avoid shellfish in the future, not that there was an overabundance of that in the mountains.

Thirty minutes later they turned off the main road onto a narrow dirt track that twisted sharply into the forested jungle. It was late in the dry season and the soil had turned to a fine dust that floated through the truck like sifted flour. To keep the red dust out, the team was forced to unfurl the canvas sides. The afternoon heat had been stifling and now that they were closed in, the temperature inside the back of the truck soon reached an intolerable level.

McShane pounded on the cab. "Chan, pull over." He'd rather walk to Burma than be broiled alive. He was sure the team would agree with him.

Chan grinned and pointed ahead. "We stop at top of hill."

McShane slumped back. Dust had begun seeping under the canvas and swirled about the enclosed truck bed. The team held their hands over noses and mouths.

Suddenly Happy Buddha drove to the side of the road and stopped. Chan got out, came around to the back, and pulled up the canvas.

"We walk now."

"'Bout goddamn time," said Pike as he dropped the tailgate and jumped to the ground.

The truck remained idling as the team quickly unloaded their rucksacks and the half-dozen boxes Chan and Happy Buddha had loaded in the truck at the Singha office. When the bed was empty, Happy Buddha steered the Nissan around and drove back down the hill. The team turned their backs, as the truck's rear tires churned up a cloud of dust.

Each of the team members grabbed one of several boxes that Chan explained contained food for the villagers. They followed Chan into the thick forest, along a wide, well-traveled trail. McShane was amazed at how similar the forest appeared to the pine forests of North Carolina.

At their first rest stop, they sat in a grove of pines. McShane asked Chan about the trees. He explained that the forests were part of a Thai government reforestation program to replace jungle that had been slashed and burned by the hill tribes. The pine seedlings were shipped from Australia.

They continued along the trail for another hour, descending the hillside into a lush valley. They crossed several mountain streams, the first water they'd seen since they began the trek. At one point they paused before an emerald pool and dipped their faces into the cool, spring-fed waters, washing away masks of red dirt from their skin.

A short distance away, they crossed a narrow bamboo bridge and entered a village tucked against the hillside. The villagers, used to trekking groups, ignored them as they passed among the bamboo huts built on teak posts. Cows, pigs, and chickens roamed freely about the small settlement. At the center of the village, Chan stopped before a hut. He lowered his rucksack, took off his shoes, and ascended the steep wooden stairs. He disappeared into a darkened room.

McShane and the team set down their boxes and crouched in the shade of the hut. Their T-shirts were saturated with sweat. They spoke quietly among themselves, mostly about the heat. McShane massaged his right calf. A muscle spasm had given him trouble since they started the trek. He really needed to exercise more.

A moment later Chan reappeared with someone else. The team gazed up the stairs as the two walked to the edge of the porch. McShane was stunned. He stared incredulously at the one person he never expected to run into again.

"Welcome to Thailand!" Rayburn gave him his best preppie smile, then descended the steps and extended his hand. "How was your trip, Sergeant McShane?"

-CHAPTER NINE-

MCSHANE UNSHOULDERED HIS RUCKSACK and let it fall to the ground. It was a good thing, he decided, that he was retiring soon, because humping a ruck was no longer the effortless endeavor it had once been. He thought back to Vietnam for a moment and recalled long, arduous forays in the jungles of Laos, and how he was barely aware of the weight on his back. Now, with a rucksack that weighed half as much, he was exhausted. Too much time sitting on a bar stool in NCO Clubs, he surmised.

McShane shook Rayburn's hand somewhat reluctantly, suspicious of his presence in the remote village. He had a sudden feeling of dread.

"This is a surprise," McShane said.

"Sergeant McShane," Rayburn said, ignoring his comment, "have your men take a load off and move out of the sun into the hut. It belongs to the headman of this Karen village, and he's been generous enough to let us use it for the night. Once they're settled, I want to brief you on the operation."

The team didn't need to be told twice to get out of the harsh sunlight. Even though it was late in the day and the sun would soon descend behind the mountains, it was still bright and intolerably hot. One by one, they climbed the steep ladder constructed of arm-size bamboo shoots. They placed the boxes of food at the top of the stairs and walked gingerly across the hut's woven bamboo-slated porch, fearful the porch would collapse under their weight. Before entering the low doorway into the thatched hut, they stopped and took off their hiking boots as was the custom in the villages and homes in Thailand.

Once inside, they moved to the far end of the hut and set down their rucks. Sunlight slanted through the openings in the bamboo thatching, casting strange patterns on the walls and floor of the nearly dark room. In the center of the room was a cook fire built on an open earthen pit surrounded by river rocks. Steam spewed from the spout of a blackened, cast iron pot. Chan went over to the pot.

"Like tea?"

The men turned toward one another with astonished looks. "Hot tea?" Colin Evans asked. "Are you serious, Chan? How 'bout a cold beer?"

Chan chuckled. "Hot tea cool you down. No shit. Villagers only have beer they keep in creek. Not very cold."

"He's right about the tea," Payne, the team medic, interjected. "It does help to cool down the body."

"I'd still rather have a beer."

"You drank all your cokes, already?" McShane asked as he entered the room.

"Yeah, 'bout an hour ago."

McShane shook his head. "Are all Southern California boys as spoiled as you, Colin?"

"You think I'm bad, you ought to meet the chicks. Nothing but attention whores, unlike the sweet, friendly ladies in North Carolina."

"Well," Payne added, "I don't know about that. I was married to a gal from Greensboro for three years, and she was the biggest shrew I've ever known. Now, as the team medic, I suggest you stay away from anything alcoholic and drink some of Chan's tea."

McShane placed his ruck in the corner of the room, and drank heartily from a plastic bottle of purified water purchased from the store where they had lunch. He watched Chan drop dried tea leaves into the pot of boiling water. He was inclined to agree with Evans. Hot tea at the moment didn't seem very appealing.

McShane found Rayburn sitting on the split teak log bench just to the left of the hut's entrance. He stared towards the mountains, at the brilliant setting sun. "Beautiful, isn't it, Sergeant McShane?"

"Yes, it is." McShane wasn't sure how he was supposed to address the young . . . whatever he was . . . CIA, or DIA, or NSA agent. Should he call him sir, Mr. Rayburn, or see how long he could go without calling him anything at all?

Rayburn stood abruptly. "Let's take a walk down to the creek. I don't have much time before I have to get back and I want to bring you up to speed on what we know."

McShane followed him down a narrow trail that skirted a small plot of vegetables. They passed several women and their children returning from the creek carrying basket loads of laundry. A little girl, barely three feet high, dressed in a faded black dress came up to him. She held out a cloth bracelet like the ones he'd seen kids weaving from strands of multi-colored thread.

"Ten baht, ten baht," she demanded.

McShane smiled and reached into his tan hiking short's pocket and pulled out a ten-baht coin. Kneeling down, he placed the coin in her outstretched hand. She then grabbed his right hand and tied the bracelet around his wrist. When she was done she turned toward Rayburn and held out another bracelet.

"Ten baht, ten baht," she again demanded.

"See what you've started, Sergeant. You just better hope none of the other kids saw you buy from her, because once you buy from one you'll have to buy from all of them." He handed her a coin, but then motioned for her to keep the bracelet. She smiled and ran to catch up to her mother.

"I'm a sucker for little kids," McShane said.

"I know what you mean. I must have a hundred of these damn things. First time in Thailand I think I bought one from every hill tribe kid who came up to me. The little girls in particular are just irresistible."

McShane was beginning to warm to Rayburn. It seemed he had a soft side and might be human after all. As they continued along the trail, McShane couldn't help but think of the Montagnard village behind their FOB in Kontum. The Karen had migrated from China and Mongolia to Burma, Thailand, and Laos centuries before, as had the Montagnards, who settled largely in Vietnam. The similarities between the two peoples were remarkable.

When they reached the swiftly moving creek, Rayburn sat on a large, flat rock at the water's edge. Two women, a few meters upstream, beat wet clothes with a bamboo stick. The Karen version of a washing machine, McShane mused. McShane sat next to Rayburn and studied the women as they repeatedly smacked the clothes.

"How would you like to wash your clothes with a stick, Steve? Can I call you Steve? Lot less formal that addressing you as Sergeant McShane."

"Sure, that's fine. 'Specially since we're supposed to be civilian tourists on a trek."

"You're right. I did call you Sergeant McShane a little while ago, didn't I? It's so serene up here you have a tendency to forget security. Well, I don't think there was any harm done. Chan is the only one who understands English, and he already knows you're in the military."

Not for long, McShane thought, as he tossed a stone into the stream. He was down to fifty-four days and a wakeup. Soon, he knew, he'd have to decide what he was going to do after he retired. Until the last few days, he hadn't given it much thought, because it never seemed like there was any hurry. By the time they finished this operation, he'd be down to about six weeks, and with thirty days accumulated leave, he really only had a couple weeks. Some of that time would be spent out-processing. Maybe he'd ask Rayburn for a job with whatever company he worked for.

"Alright, let me bring you up to speed on what we know about Slade. A Caucasian was spotted a few days ago by a Thai army helicopter searching for Burmese soldiers. Apparently, this fellow was with a group of what was believed to be KNU guerrillas. The spotter in the chopper had the pilot turn around for another look. He managed to take a picture of the guy before he ducked into the woods with the Karen." Rayburn reached into his shirt pocket and pulled out a photograph. "This is a copy of that photo. Take a look and tell me what you think."

McShane was a little apprehensive. It had been over twenty years since Slade's disappearance. He wasn't sure how he'd react if, in fact, the picture was of Slade. He was struck with a flood of emotions, and his mind tumbled back to that overcast afternoon in 1970 when his Bright Light team learned that Slade's entire team had been wiped out and Slade captured. When the war officially ended and all the prisoners were supposedly returned in 1973, he waited anxiously to see if Slade showed up. For several years afterwards he expected any day for Slade to walk through his team room door. By the late '70s, he'd given up. Now, out of the blue, he finds out Slade may be alive.

As he hesitantly took the photograph from Rayburn's outstretched hand, he swallowed hard, not knowing what to expect. He studied the picture carefully, but no matter how closely he looked at the blurred image of the bearded man standing amongst the Karen, he could not identify the man in the picture. He was disappointed. He wanted to get to the bottom of the mystery, and this only deepened it. Who was the man in the photo? And what was he doing fighting with the KNU?

"Sorry, can't tell from this. It's out of focus, and even if it were clear, I doubt I could identify him twenty years later, with a beard. It's been too damn long. Maybe, if he were clean shaven and sitting as close to me as I am to you."

Rayburn shrugged his shoulders. "Well, you're right. It is a shitty picture. All it does is show a tall white guy standing around with some short Karen hill tribesmen. I didn't think you'd be able to identify him, which brings us to why you're here in the first place."

Rayburn watched as McShane tossed another small rock out into the water then turned and faced him. "All along, what we've wanted is to find this guy, pull him out, and properly identify him. If he's just some guy who feels compelled to help the KNU, for whatever reason, then fine."

McShane looked at Rayburn curiously. "Do you have reason to believe there are mercenaries helping the KNU?"

"There's an American missionary in Naisoi. He told me a couple months back that there's a Canadian who comes over every so often, and stays with him and his family. According to the missionary, the man claims to be a former Canadian paratrooper, trained in explosives. He disappears across the border for two to three weeks then goes back to Canada, only to return months later. Mercenary? He doesn't get paid. Tourist who likes to live dangerously? I don't know. Maybe the guy in the photo is the Canadian. Maybe not."

Suddenly, Rayburn's train of thought was disrupted by one of the women washing clothes when she hollered at a little girl swimming in the water. He stared at her for a moment then dropped his head, trying to recall what he'd wanted to say.

McShane took the opportunity to yawn quietly, covering his mouth with his hand. He didn't want Rayburn to think he was bored. On the contrary, what Rayburn had to say was fascinating. He was just beat, not only from the heat, but from not having fully recovered from the seventeen-hour flight and the loss of a day when they crossed the International Date Line.

Rayburn lifted his head slowly. "What I do know is that the Senate Sub-Committee looking into the MIA/POW sightings is anxious as hell to find out if this one is legitimate. To date, all the other sightings have proven to be bogus. Unlike the others, however, there's a lot of evidence backing up this one."

"And that's why you want my team to go in," McShane added. "To check it out."

"Correct. And if it's a credible sighting and proves to be Slade, pull him out, whether he wants to go, or not."

McShane didn't like the last part of Rayburn's statement. Slade had been missing for twenty-two years. He had no wife, or children, or living family. McShane doubted there was anybody alive, except maybe Rayburn and the Sub-Committee, who gave a shit. Sure, it might be interesting to learn what he'd been up to. But, in McShane's opinion, the old saying about letting sleeping dogs lie applied here.

"And if he absolutely refuses?"

"Use your imagination, but bring him in. Lot of folks in Washington would love to talk to him. But let's not jump to conclusions. It's probably only the Canadian, or some misguided mercenary or drug runner, using the KNU for his own private army."

"Let's hope so," McShane said.

Rayburn brushed off his tan cargo pants and started to stand. "A few days ago, after you met with Chan in Bangkok, he spoke with some KNU soldiers he knows. When he questioned them about the Caucasian, they told him they knew where his village was. It's about a two day trek from here, over that mountain range." Rayburn pointed to a saw-toothed-shaped ridge beyond the creek.

McShane followed Rayburn's finger and closely scrutinized the steep, heavily forested peak. It reminded him of the same eerie terrain he'd cursed countless times in Laos. Was trekking into the thick Burmese jungles how he'd envisioned spending his final weeks in the military? Not hardly.

Rayburn stood and arched his back. "Tomorrow, at first light, Chan and a KNU soldier from this village will lead you and your men into those mountains. The soldier who knows the KNU camp will guide you. Use the trek cover story. Chan will tell the KNU you're lost, and ask if you can stay for the night. Hopefully, our guy will be there and you can befriend him and learn his identity. If he's anyone other than Slade, leave him alone. The Sub-committee only cares about Slade. Any questions?"

McShane got up and stretched. He was suddenly stiff and sore from the ride in the truck and the hike into the mountain valley. Just another reminder of why he was hanging up his jump helmet.

"Are we still going to train the KNU soldiers? We're supposed to call for an airdrop of weapons and ammo when we get there."

Rayburn turned to walk back up to the trail. "Play that one by ear. If there's an opportunity, then give them some training. They're already pretty damn experienced. The KNU have been fighting for their independence for over forty years. As for weapons, we have three hundred folding-stock AK-74s, a dozen RPDs, and a half dozen RPG-7s, with thousands of rounds still in the original boxes we liberated from Iraq during the Gulf War. When you make contact with the villagers, just give us the word and we'll air drop everything. There's also freeze-dried rations and medicine packed and ready to go."

"That at ought to help the cause."

"Well, it's not much to our way of thinking, but for them, it's huge."

McShane followed Rayburn up the path. The sun had already set behind the mountains, and the cloudless sky slowly turned a vibrant orange. The temperature had also dropped several degrees, another similarity to Laos and perhaps another reason to take caution. Nothing was ever as it seemed in Laos. He wondered if Burma was the same way.

On the walk back to the hut, his thoughts again turned to the Bright Light mission. It had been such a disappointment not to find any of the American team alive. Or even their bodies.

Lap's eyewitness account of the team's deaths had been devastating to everyone on the Bright Light team. He knew Lap, Slade's most experienced and trusted indig, was a superb soldier. But when they couldn't find any trace of Mullins, Lofton, or Broderick, and when Lap, who'd conveniently showed up after the team's arrival, couldn't account for his time after becoming separated from Slade, and couldn't tell them where he'd seen the men killed, he became suspicions about the wiry Cambodian.

McShane suspected Lap had cowered in the jungle, perhaps self-inflicting the wound to his arm, knowing full well that help would eventually arrive. Or worse yet, he had somehow colluded with the NVA. It was an unspeakable thought, one he had never brought up at the time, because he couldn't bring himself to believe it. Whatever the circumstances, his suspicions deepened once they returned to the FOB. The next morning, Lap abruptly quit, turning in all his equipment.

Lap left without taking a single personal possession. He was certain Lap feared for his life, knowing full well that if the truth came out about his cowardice, or what he knew about the disappearance of the team, he would be killed.

A few years after the war ended, the Laotian Government had allowed a Joint Casualty Recovery Team access to the area. Assisted by local villagers, some of whom claimed to have been living in Muong May at the time, they searched for remains for a week.

The only remains they dug up were those of a long deceased water buffalo, and several pigs. The team was still listed as MIA.

McShane's attention returned to the present, and he reflected on Rayburn's photograph. If the person in the picture was Slade, and he was in the KNU camp, then he'd be able to fill in the missing pieces. Otherwise, he knew, the events of that horrid day twenty-two years ago would forever remain a mystery.

- CHAPTER TEN -

PRU SCRAMBLED OVER THE narrow, rocky ledge. Worn smooth from centuries of rain and wind, the ledge was at the base of a craggy, three-hundred foot, vine-covered cliff. A late morning drizzle had dampened the rocks. Carrying the squad's Chinese-made RPD light machine gun by the handle in his left hand and an ammo can in the other, Pru moved cautiously over the slick stone surface until he found protection behind a chest-high boulder among an outcropping of rocks.

He paused to catch his breath then leaned over the rock and took a long sweeping glance along the trail forty meters below. He grinned. The fields of fire were perfect, he calculated.

Turning around, he studied the rock mass behind him. It cast a dark shadow over his position. He knew of at least a half dozen caves hidden behind the vines; caves used by the Red Karen over the years for shelter from monsoon storms or refuge from their enemies. If the need arose, he, too, could seek sanctuary.

He positioned the barrel of RPD in between a pair of basketball-sized rocks and began unraveling linked belts of 7.62 rounds from the ammo can. Loading the first round into the chamber of the machine gun, he quietly snapped the bolt cover in place. The Burmese army patrol they'd spotted earlier should be along any moment, he guessed. His squad had had to hurry to intercept the patrol. He sat against the wet rocks and waited for his squad and the American who'd trained him so well.

Pru closed his eyes for a moment. He was tired. They'd been dodging Burmese patrols throughout the morning and into the afternoon. This had been going on for three days. Even though Thailand had increased its attacks against the invading Burmese, it seemed there were Burmese patrols searching for them at every bend in the trail. This would be the squad's first chance for an ambush in several days. Their last ambush was against a fifteen-man patrol, in which they had killed or severely wounded everyone. But they'd paid a price. The Burmese had chased them relentlessly, forcing them to retreat deep into the mountains and across the border into Thailand.

His thoughts drifted back to the day he turned seventeen, three years before, when a Karen National Union recruiter came to his village. The KNU soldier brandished a new AK-74 with a folding metal stock. He said he'd taken it from a dead Burmese soldier. Pru had stared at him in awe, impressed by the soldier's plea for volunteer recruits. All the males in the village old enough enlisted. Pru and the other recruits were hailed as heroes by the villagers that day. He had been proud. All he'd wanted to do was kill Burmese. But after three years, he'd grown weary of the fighting. His greatest wish now was that the fighting end and his people regain their freedom and be secure in their own land.

A sudden sound from below focused his attention on the trail. Peering over the rock, he studied its length. A hundred meters away, the point man for the Burmese army patrol was approaching. The soldier, Pru could tell, was not paying attention. Instead of keeping an eye out for Pru's squad, he was looking down at his feet as he walked. This was going to be too easy, he thought.

Pru glanced to his left, wondering where his squad was. If he had to, he'd ambush the patrol on his own. He'd let the point man pass his position then open up on the main body. Before they had a chance to react, he'd be long gone, hiding in a cave. He sneaked a look at the clump of vines behind him, where there was a narrow opening in the rocks that twisted deep into the mountain and ended in a vast chamber. More than once, he'd hidden in the cave during storms.

The point man was almost directly below him now. He could see the rest of the patrol about thirty meters behind him. His pulse quickened. Finally, the soldier disappeared from view. He took aim through the RPDs sights. He would wait a little longer, until the patrol entered the kill zone. While he waited, he placed three grenades next to the RPD.

Stumbling often on the narrow dirt trail, the soldiers seemed tired and listless to Pru. He chuckled to himself over their sloppy ways. The twenty or so soldiers were bunched up, barely half a meter between each man. He almost felt sympathy for them. They would die too easily, without much of a fight. But then he remembered what the American had told him once when they killed several soldiers in an ambush, "Better them than us." Over the years, he'd seen too many of his own people killed. Today would even the score a little.

The afternoon was hot and humid. Pru licked his lips as he wiped the sweat from his brow. He was suddenly thirsty and cursed himself for not taking a drink earlier. But he knew this wouldn't take long. He could drink all he wanted inside the cave.

The patrol was near enough now. He forgot his squad. He could handle this on his own. He adjusted the rear sights, fixing the V of the front sight post on the chest of the lead man in the file. The soldier looked so young, Pru thought. It saddened him a little to think the soldier would be dead soon and never experience life further. At least Pru understood why he was fighting. The Burmese soldiers didn't understand at all. And as a Burmese conscript, you didn't ask questions.

Pru moved the selector switch on his RPD from safe to auto. He'd wait a moment more, until the lead man and at least six soldiers more had rounded the bend and were out in the open, in his kill zone. He took a deep breath and stroked the trigger with his index finger.

Suddenly, he was flooded with thoughts of his wife, Maw. He'd only seen her twice since the village headman had married them six months before. Hopefully, he'd soon be able to return to his village in the lush mountain valley in southern Burma, and begin having children. But he feared the war would never end, and that day may never come. He squeezed the trigger.

The RPD bucked slightly as he opened fire. He swept the muzzle slowly along the length of the exposed Burmese file. The din of machine gun fire reverberating off the rock cliff was deafening, but he didn't notice. Relishing the moment, he allowed the burst to go on longer than he should.

A ripple of confusion and panic immediately spread through the patrol as one by one their comrades were struck down. The young soldier at the front of the file was nearly torn in half. The next half dozen soldiers perished within moments of Pru opening fire. The anguished cries of the wounded echoed through the forest. But Pru was too absorbed in bloodletting to hear them. The patrol quickly became a shredded mass.

Pru finally forced himself to stop. The stench of cordite hung in the air like a mist on a cold morning. He scanned the carnage. In disbelief, he noticed a few soldiers huddled behind a tree. They were crying like newborns. They'd never even returned fire, choosing instead to cower like mongrel pups. They didn't deserve to live. He trained his weapon on the cowards and opened fire.

Suddenly, Pru felt a hand on his shoulder and he pulled his finger away from the trigger. He turned and stared upward into the American's blue eyes.

"That's enough, Pru," he said in Karen. His voice was calm and soothing. "You have done well. They are all dead. Save the bullets for the living." He knew Pru was charged with a rush of adrenaline, common during a firefight. He'd enjoyed that high himself many times.

"I am sorry I did not wait," Pru said apologetically. "I did not want the patrol to get away, Mr. Slade."

"It is all right, Pru. Nuua twisted his ankle, and we stopped to wrap it. We must hurry. Maybe more

Burmese come. Shan and the men gather the dead soldier's rifles and equipment."

Slade held back as Pru scrambled down the rocks. Slade kept the RPD trained on the trail in the event another Burmese patrol showed up to investigate the gunfire.

Pru joined Shan and the other ten Karen guerrillas in his squad as they quickly went from body to body, collecting as many weapons and magazines as they could. Pru noticed during the search that none of the soldiers carried food. The Burmese base camp must be nearby, he guessed.

Shan was from the same village as Pru and had been fighting with the KNU for five years. Shan had become Slade's most trusted soldier, acting as squad leader and instructor to new recruits. He was particularly fond of Pru because of his dedication to the cause of ridding the Burmese from their homeland. Also, because Pru had married his sister, Maw.

"Pru, come here," his brother-in-law said. His voice was full of excitement.

Pru kicked the body he'd been searching over the side of the hill and walked over to Shan. His brother-in-law was kneeling by a body lying face down in a pool of blood.

"I found this in his pack!" Shan exclaimed, holding out a spiral notebook. Pru took it from him, then stood over the corpse and studied it curiously.

Using the toe of his boot, Pru pried the body over onto its back. The dead man's appearance surprised him. He was gray-haired and grossly overweight. It was impossible to tell his age, because his face had been torn away by an RPD round. Dressed in the standard green Burmese army fatigues, he wore no rank. He thumbed through the pages of the notebook. He couldn't read Burmese, but Luan, their assistant squad leader could.

With great interest, Slade watched Pru as he went through the pockets of the fat man. Compared to the other soldiers, small and frail in their baggy uniforms, he seemed out of place, his belly billowing out of his shirt. He also wondered what was in the notebook Pru thumbed through. Unable to stand back and idly look on, Slade climbed down the rocks and walked up the trail toward Pru.

"Mr. Slade," Pru said, pointing to the portly corpse. "He no soldier."

Slade took a deep breath, avoiding glancing at the man's disfigured face, and knelt by the body. He ran his gaze the length of the corpse. His attention focused on the man's right hand. Careful not to touch the bloodied hand, he held it up by the shirt sleeve. Slade yanked the green bandana from around the man's neck and wiped the blood away from the fingers. On each of his fingers was a thick gold ring embedded with magnificent, multi-faceted rubies and sapphires. The man was obviously of great wealth, Slade decided, and definitely no soldier.

The buttons on the man's shirt strained to contain his gut, but Slade felt there was more to his obesity than fat. Slade took a Swiss Army knife from his pocket and in one swift motion ran the knife blade the length of the shirt, cutting away the buttons. He grinned. Tied around his waist was a canvas bag, bulging at the seams.

"I wonder what our fat friend is carrying in the bag?" Slade muttered to himself. "Been working two jobs, maybe?"

Slade made an incision the length of the bag with the tip of the blade, slicing it nearly in half. He spread the two halves apart, revealing the contents of the bag. He picked up one of the half-dozen clear plastic bags that had been stuffed inside, and held it up in the light.

No stranger to heroin, Slade wasn't all that shocked by the brown powder inside the bags. For six years after he'd escaped from his NVA captors, he'd lived and fought with his rescuers, remnants of a Special Forces and CIA trained Meo guerrilla force in Laos. The Meo had taken to the mountainous regions of northwestern Laos after the Vietnam conflict. From hidden jungle sanctuaries, the guerrillas continued their own war against the Pathet Lao, the Laotian communists who'd allied themselves with the North Vietnamese during the war years.

To support their war, they'd cultivated opium poppies on small, clandestine plots in the mountain valleys near their villages. After the poppies were harvested, they were processed into nearly pure heroin in secret jungle labs. The heroin was then traded to agents acting on behalf of drug syndicates from Thailand, for weapons and medicine. On more than one occasion, he'd visited the clandestine labs with Meo leaders.

It was no secret to him where the heroin was likely to end up – on the streets of major U.S. cities. Unfortunately, without the heroin, they never would have been able to carry on their fight. While never approving of the Meos' money making ventures, he wrote them off as the cost of doing business.

"So," Slade said, "the Burmese army is running drugs on the side, huh? Bet you aren't even in the army, are you?" He felt Shan's hand on his shoulder and looked up.

"We must go, Mr. Slade. Luan heard a helicopter in the valley below. We take drugs and his rings with us. Can trade for medicine and many weapons."

Slade stood slowly, a frown firmly etched into his forehead. The thought of being party to dealing drugs still bothered him. Well, he'd just have to look the other way and think of all the good the money would bring to the Karen people. With any luck at all, the drugs would be confiscated by police before they made it to the street.

The squad quickly moved off the trail and scrambled up the rocks, taking cover behind the same outcropping where Pru had made his ambush. Pru took up a position behind the RPD and pointed it skyward. The whop-whop of two Royal Thai helicopters grew steadily louder as they traversed the mountainside. They waited patiently for the vintage Hueys to pass, but instead they flew directly toward them.

Pru grabbed the RPD by the carrying handle and led the squad into the cave entrance beneath the vines. He shone his U.S. Army surplus, crook-necked flashlight into the darkness and began to descend into the depths of the cave, the squad following closely behind. The cavern walls were narrow, rubbing against the Karens' shoulders. Soon, others in the squad brought out their lights.

Slade shone the Maglite he'd purchased on a trip to Chiang Mai onto the claustrophobic limestone walls that soared upwards into the darkness, and marveled at nature's handiwork. They were walking, he realized, into the heart of the cave through a massive fissure, formed countless millions of years ago. The cavern pressed in even more, causing him to walk sideways. The limestone pressed into his skin. He felt as though his chest would collapse under the pressure. Suddenly, a bat swooped down from its perch and brushed against his cheek. Unprepared for the intrusion, he nearly shrieked in terror.

Just when he felt he couldn't take another step, the passage abruptly widened into a domed room. A sliver of light slanted from a fissure in the dome's ceiling, illuminating the room in an eerie, dull light. Gradually, his eyes grew accustomed to the soft light and he turned off the Maglite. The squad was already lowering their packs and finding places to sit.

Slade glanced at the luminous dials of his watch. It was 1800 hours. They'd been on the move since first light, close to thirteen hours. He suddenly felt very tired and realized he was nearing complete exhaustion. Unshouldering his ruck, he tossed it against the cave wall near the rear of the chamber. He walked over to Shan, who stood a short distance away, gazing up at the narrow beam of daylight, and rested his hand on the Karen's shoulder.

"We will stay here for the night," Slade said. "There are still two hours of light left. The Burmese will be looking for their men and the Thais will be looking for the Burmese. They will never find us here."

Shan nodded and tossed his ruck next to Slade's. "Yes, but I will have Pru guard the entrance to be safe."

Slade would also insist each squad member stand guard for an hour, until first light, at which time they'd return to their base camp, nearly two days of tough trekking from the cave.

Slade sat down next to his pack. The cave was surprisingly cool, and he shivered. He looked forward to returning to the camp. They had been on hit-and-run operations for a week, an unusually long time. Rarely did they stay out for more than four or five days. The Karen guerrillas kept their wives with them at their secret base camp, and if kept apart for too long, the men lost their desire to fight.

He closed his eyes. The sudden change in temperature in the cave triggered memories of the chilled waters of the Kamon River. He allowed his thoughts to drift back to that day, some twenty plus years before, when he'd been pulled from the water by the Meo.

After the guerrillas brought him to shore, they'd half dragged, half carried him through the treacherous Laotian jungle. At the time, he hadn't realized he'd been wounded in the leg by a piece of shrapnel from one of the gunship's rockets. After a while, since he was unable to walk on his own, the hill tribesmen built a litter out of bamboo poles and carried him.

What he still vividly recalled were the jungle nights, when the temperature dropped forty degrees below the daytime high. Dressed only in his tattered jungle fatigues, he lie awake most nights, shivering uncontrollably on a bamboo mat. Delirious from an infection that had rapidly spread from the leg wound, and with no knowledge of the Meo language, he was unable to communicate his discomfort.

The days hadn't been much better. Lapsing in and out of unconsciousness, he was unable to ward off the swarms of mosquitoes that fed on his exposed flesh, until his arms were covered in welts, and his face was so swollen he could barely open his eyes.

After four days, they reached the Meo village, huddled at the base of a jagged mountain. They put him in the headman's hut. The headman's wife, with some assistance from their three children, replaced his fatigues with heavy, black, hand-woven tribal clothing. Each night, to ward off the mountain chill, they built a fire in an earthen pit located in the center of the hut. For the first few days, either the wife or one of the children hand fed him a broth made from roots and boiled vegetables. By week's end, he was able to feed himself, and was eating solid food, primarily rice and vegetables with bits of chicken or pork.

Two weeks after arriving in the village, he ventured outside the hut. The headman had fashioned a crutch for him from a forked tree limb. His oldest daughter, Phra, a beautiful young woman with high cheek bones, jet black hair that fell to her waist, and almond eyes, walked a few feet behind to offer assistance if needed. That first day he'd tired quickly, and returned to the hut after only walking a short distance.

It was also Phra who usually changed his dressings. He recalled her gentleness, her constant smile, and unusually white teeth: it was a common practice among hill tribe women to chew the mildly narcotic betel nut, staining their teeth and gums black. After cleansing the wound in his shoulder and leg, she rubbed a putrid smelling black salve over the wounds. Whatever was in the concoction worked, because his injuries healed quickly.

Slowly, his strength and mobility increased until he no longer depended on the crutch. His trips around the village grew longer. Except for a few women, who had remained behind to take care of the smaller children, and a few men to stand guard, the village was deserted. The remainder of the men and women worked in the rice fields. Many of the younger men, who were members of the village militia, patrolled the mountain trails around the village. However, the Pathet Lao rarely ventured into this mountain valley, and the men usually spent their time hunting game.

Sometimes Phra stayed behind to help her mother while her father and two younger brothers worked the fields. On those occasions, she accompanied him on his walks. They never spoke, but he enjoyed her company and engaging smile. His spirits soared when she was there. Usually they strolled to the creek and sat on a flat boulder that jutted out into the water. They dangled their feet into the chilled waters of the rushing stream. On their first trip to the creek, he'd taught her how to skip a rock. In return, she taught him the fine art of washing clothes in the creek. She quickly became adept at her new skill, often out-skipping him. On the other hand, he frequently mimed an excuse when she handed him a pile of dirty clothes.

Near the end of his fourth week in the village, he was awakened just before dawn by the clatter of automatic weapons fire. He'd almost forgotten what the sound was like. He hurriedly pulled on his jungle boots, the only piece of original GI issue clothing remaining. The headman handed him a Chinese-made bolt action SKS rifle and two clips of ammo. He motioned him to follow.

Off to the west, the mountain ridges were just beginning to redden as the sun started its ascent. In the twilight, he made out the women and children scampering into the forest to the caves. There was a sense of urgency, but it looked like they'd been through the drill before. He didn't see Phra and hoped she was safe with her mother and brothers.

The gunfire came from the west, across the stream. The hill tribe men, all carrying SKSs, rushed toward the creek. Slapping one of the seven-round clips into his own ancient SKS, he limped off in the direction of the stream, glancing around one last time for Phra.

The village was nearly deserted as he zigzagged his way among the huts. He'd lost sight of the headman. A few stragglers, mostly mothers gathering up their children and some elderly, were trying to make it into the forest. Unsure if the village was under attack or not, he moved among the shadows, keeping a wary eye out for intruders.

By the time he reached the narrow wooden bridge that crossed the water, the firing had ceased. A mule-drawn cart suddenly appeared on the other side and started across the bridge. It was moving fast and the clatter of the wood wheels against the hollow bamboo cross pieces was deafening. The driver beat the animal furiously with a long frayed bamboo shaft, trying to force the skinny beast to move even faster. As the wagon passed, he saw several bodies piled in the back. They were awash in blood.

A burst of automatic weapons fire diverted his attention to the wood line on the other side of the creek. The gunfire was intense. He guessed there were at least a dozen weapons firing simultaneously. Rather than cross the bridge and risk being shot, he waded across the stream, into the brush covering the creek bank. He grasped a low overhanging branch and pulled himself up into a tangle of underbrush. He peered through the bushes. The firing had suddenly ceased.

Village men emerged from the trees and retreated across the one-lane dirt road that led to the bridge. It was light enough now that he could make out features. He recognized many of the men. They were dragging bodies by the hands and feet as they pulled back. Bodies littered the road. As he watched, it was obvious they'd tangled with a force far superior than their own. Either North Vietnamese or Pathet Lao, armed with fully automatic AK-47s and RPD light machine guns. It had been a slaughter.

He crawled cautiously out of the brush to a wounded villager, pulling himself along the road with his hands. He recognized the teenage Meo as the eldest son of the headman's brother, who lived in the hut behind him. He'd often seen the boy washing his younger sister and brother at the creek.

His gaze traveled the length of the boy's bare back, over the black loincloth, settling on where his legs had once been. They'd both been severed above the knee. A trail of blood marked his path from the trees. The boy reached out to him. His tortured eyes, pleading for help, fixed on him. There was nothing he could do. Death was certain. He cradled the boys head in his lap. Suddenly, his frail body shuddered then went limp. His head lolled to the side. Eyes, now vacant, stared off towards the creek, at nothing.

He gently laid the boys head on the dirt road and then stood. There was a bitter taste in his mouth. He took a deep breath and looked around. The remnants of the ill-trained and ill-equipped militia tended the wounded, gathered their dead. Seeing the militia in such disarray, he thought there must be something he could do, a way to repay the villagers for saving his life. Then, in an instant, he realized what he had to do. It was what he had been trained to do. Somehow, he would communicate to the headman that he wished to remain in the village to train his people to fight their enemies more effectively.

He helped a villager with a jagged shoulder wound across the bridge to a makeshift dispensary set up in the ceremonial hut. The women and children had returned and he was pleased to see Phra unharmed, tending to the needs of the wounded. Wives and mothers carried the dead, some twenty or so males, back to their individual huts to prepare them for burial.

He did what he could to help with the wounded. Of course, there were no modern medicines: those had very likely been depleted years before, once their Special Forces trainers returned to Okinawa and the United States. But they seemed to do fine with their own jungle medicine, perfected over the centuries.

He didn't have to ask the headman to stay. The headman, in a most unusual manner, asked him. The morning after the firefight, the headman led him to a vacant hut, gave him an iron pot and some bowls. He motioned him up the bamboo stairs then walked away. When he entered the hut, he found a bamboo mat with a tattered U.S. Army blanket folded on top. A fire blazed in the fire pit. Next to the pit were two baskets, one filled with rice and the other fresh vegetables. He had taken the gesture as a yes, and quickly set up house with his new possessions.

The next morning, he awoke to the chatter of hushed voices. For a time he was disoriented in his new surroundings. Dressing quickly, he went outside to investigate. He was stunned. Three loosely formed ranks of grinning villagers stood at attention. Each held a weapon, mostly SKSs, but a few AKs, acquired after the firefight, at shoulder arms. He stood at the top of the stairs and grinned back, thinking of all the hard work that lay ahead.

An hour later, he began conducting the first of what was to become daily training exercises with his rag-tag army. They appeared unsightly and ill-trained, but, over the course of the next several days, it became clear that many still remembered much of what they'd been taught by their SF trainers. Their marksmanship was superb. They could track and move about the jungle forests with animal stealth. And, more importantly, they were fearless. They had just been outgunned during the firefight, he realized, although far more of the NVA had been killed than villagers. Many of the enemy, he later learned, were hunted down and killed.

It wasn't long before he led them on forays into North Vietnamese Army and Pathet Lao sanctuaries to conduct ambushes. They were careful only to attack enemy positions that were a minimum of a two-day trek from their village, thus protecting their anonymity and significantly reducing the chance of a counterattack. In just a few months, they had replaced their older semi-automatic SKSs with fully automatic AKs and confiscated a half-dozen RPD light machine guns, two older RPG-2 shoulder-fired rocket launchers, scores of grenades, and thousands of 7.62mm rounds. Under his guidance, the village militia was transformed into a formidable fighting force, to be admired and feared.

During those months, he slowly and painstakingly learned to speak Meo. Eventually, his vocabulary increased until he could effectively communicate with his men, using a combination of Meo and sign language.

Once able to understand their language, he learned that the NVA who'd attacked the village had stumbled on them accidentally. The NVA's guide, a Meo who had been forcibly conscripted after his family was killed, and had now joined the village militia, explained he had become lost, and led them into the village accidentally. He was from a village many miles away, and had never traveled more than a few miles from his home.

When he wasn't out in the field with his men, Phra often came to his hut and cooked his meals. It was clear that she was grateful for what he was doing. She helped him with Meo, and he taught her some English. Soon, using a mixture of both languages, they were able to converse with relative ease. They formed a close bond, but he resisted the urge to carry the relationship any further, if only because he knew he would be leaving someday. At the time, he hadn't realized he'd live in the village for the next six years.

While he never again quite experienced the bitter cold of those first few nights traveling through the Laotian jungle, he never forgot his years living among the Meo. He hoped they were now living in peace and that Phra had married and started a family.

Shan nudged Slade in the side, jolting him away from his thoughts. He held a sheet of paper up to his flashlight.

"Yes, Shan."

"Soldier we kill with drugs?"

"Yes, go on." Slade urged.

"He not really soldier, but agent work for Burmese government in Mandalay. These papers in Thai and Burmese. Papers say it okay for him to go to both countries. Also give him protection. This man very important. Visas for both countries difficult. Must have political friends. I think maybe he a spy for. . ."

"Shan," Slade interrupted, "he was a drug runner, pure and simple." He was weary from the long, stressful day and only wanted to sleep, not discuss the fat man. "I am certain he had friends in both governments, probably also drug runners, but he was selling the heroin in Thailand, probably for American money, and taking the money back to Burma to buy guns on the open market. Really, it is no different from what you're going to do. You should thank him."

Somewhat disappointed in Slade's lack of interest, Shan reluctantly shoved the papers back into the pouch the man had carried and walked away. Slade stretched out inside his Thai army sleeping bag, bought from an outdoor vender in Chiang Mai, and immediately fell asleep.

- CHAPTER ELEVEN -

CHAN WAS UP BEFORE first light, boiling two-dozen eggs he'd purchased from the headman the night before. From years of leading hill tribe treks into the mountains, he knew Americans loved to start out their day with eggs. Normally, he'd only hard boil a dozen eggs, but judging from these Americans' size, and seeing their large appetites at the roadside restaurant the day before, he knew they ate a lot.

McShane awakened when he heard Chan blow his nose. That was one thing he'd noticed about the Thais, they were constantly blowing their noses. No doubt, he surmised, because of all the dust in the air during the dry season. He ran his hands through his hair, put on his 49er cap, picked his way through his sleeping teammates to the stairs and then to the cook-fire, and squatted next to Chan.

"Morning, Chan."

Chan grinned. "Make eggs for you and your men. Big day, today." Chan rubbed his face with the back of his right hand, as if in deep thought. "Maybe walk eight, ten hours before we stop to rest and sleep." Then he added casually, "Very hot, very hot."

McShane didn't need to be reminded what the weather was going to be like. He had dreaded it even before he dozed off last night. He thought that after all these years of living and fighting in warm climates he'd have grown accustomed to the heat. But, he hadn't, which is why he contemplated retiring to Alaska. But then he had remembered he didn't like extreme cold either. Someplace on California's Central Coast had been another thought. Perhaps Big Sur, where he'd spent a memorable week the summer after high school. Well, he still had several weeks to think about it. Perhaps he'd check out a couple places during his leave.

An hour later, the team left the tranquil village and followed Chan and Tah, the KNU soldier, down a dusty path toward the creek. They hopscotched across exposed rocks in the stream, and picked up the trail on the other side.

McShane glanced up at the formidable mountain peak that was their first obstacle before entering Burma. He swore to himself. It was cool now, but it wouldn't be long before the weather would turn insufferable. Yep, he thought, Chan was right. This was going to be a "big day".

By late-morning, it was sweltering-hot and the sun hammered mercilessly at the team as they ascended the steep mountain trail. Thankfully, they were nearing the crest. The trail had been one endless switch back, taking them from one end of the mountain to the next. Back and forth, back and forth they had traveled, through a dank, jungle landscape that never varied.

When they finally crested the mountain peak, they stopped to take a break in a thicket of dense pine trees, the first real change in the flora. Exhausted, McShane dropped his rucksack and sat with his back against one of the pines. Pike sat next to him. They both drank from their water bottles. Both stared up at the tall, thin trees.

"Pine trees in Thailand?" Pike asked.

"Chan said that because the Karen had slashed and burned so much of the jungle for agriculture that the Aussie government sent over pine seedlings as part of a reforestation program. They seemed to have taken to the Thai climate."

"In Burma soon," Chan said as he knelt in front of McShane. "Have lunch, now. Stay at Karen village in valley for the night."

"Sounds good." Pike said.

Tah started a fire then brought out a large pot from his canvas rucksack. There was a small spring nearby. He filled the pot half full of water then placed it on the fire. Once the water was boiling, he scooped out several handfuls of rice from a burlap sack and dumped them in the pot. Chan used a flat rock for a cutting board, and began chopping carrots and cabbage.

"Oh, shit," Pike spat out. "Rice and fuckin' vegetables again."

Chan had made rice with vegetables and pork the previous evening. Everyone on the team had agreed it was delicious, and devoured the large bowls of food, particularly Pike, who couldn't seem to get enough.

"The way you ate last night, I thought you loved the stuff?" McShane said.

"Yeah, but twice in twenty-four hours?"

Lieutenant Hansen sat across from Pike with Everett, Evans, and Payne. "You'd better get used to it," Hansen said. "Because that's what these people eat and it's all any of us are going to have for the next several days. So, if you want to starve, be my guest. If you hold us up in any way because you're too weak to walk because you're malnourished, I'll have McShane shoot your ass and dump your sorry pathetic, piece of shit body over the cliff."

Everyone on the team, including Pike, laughed. "Alright, alright, you made your point, L.T. I'll shut up."

When Chan dished out the food, all eyes were on Pike, waiting for his reaction. Without complaint, he took his bowl of the rice/vegetable concoction with a grin and ate more than his share of Chan's lunch.

An hour later, they picked up their packs and followed Chan and Tah down the slope. McShane could understand why the on-again, off-again border war between Thailand and Burma had gone on for so long. When a mountain ridge was the only borderline dividing two countries, there was plenty of room for misinterpretation. Burma could always claim that their border was the next ridge over, or vice versa. It wasn't like there was a WELCOME TO BURMA sign posted at the border.

As the afternoon wore on, the air grew even hotter, and more humid. The trail was fainter and more treacherous on the Burmese side of the border. The team had to watch their steps on the rocky path. Chan, who had never traveled beyond the village where they'd spent the previous night, wandered off the path a number of times. Finally, he allowed Tah to take over the lead.

The landscape abruptly changed as they began to ascend yet another mountain peak. The path broadened into a narrow road-sized trail and, from the footprints in the dirt, appeared well-traveled. Large boulders lined both sides of the road. Craggy rock cliffs, covered in thick vines, loomed over them. McShane noticed several caves scattered about the unusual rock formations. What a great spot for an ambush, he noted.

Tah had been several meters ahead, followed by McShane then Lieutenant Hansen, Colin Evans, Charlie Pike, Travis Payne, Wade Everett, and finally Chan. Abruptly, Tah stopped and knelt. McShane and Hansen sped ahead to join him.

McShane crouched next to Tah and was stunned by what he saw. In plain view, just off the side of the trail, was a bloated leg, severed just above the knee. The stench from the decaying leg nearly caused him to gag.

"What do you think, Steve?" Hansen asked. The other team members had now caught up and stared down at the grizzly sight.

McShane studied the boot and bit of clothing left on the leg closely. He moved it around with a tree limb. Scores of maggots poured from the stump. "Well, L.T., I'd say judging by the military style boot and green fatigues that this leg once belonged to a soldier. Probably a Burmese soldier."

He stood and glanced around the road. Something else caught his attention, and he walked over to a spot in the dirt. The team followed to a broad expanse of what appeared to be coagulating blood.

"Judging by all the dried blood here, several others may have been killed. Let's look around and see what we find."

Wade Everett noticed a blood trail leading over the edge of the slope. Colin Evans was behind him. "Hey, Colin, check this out." His voice crackled with excitement.

"What'd ya got, Wade?" Evans asked.

Everett was now a half-dozen feet down the edge. "More bodies. Three more in fact." He bent down over one of the corpses and ripped the collar off the shirt, then climbed back up.

Everyone gathered around Everett to see what he'd found. He held out the piece of collar. Tah took it in his hands, smiled, and uttered something to Chan in Karen. Chan nodded his head and grinned.

"He say patch on shirt belong to sergeant in Burma army. Say killed by KNU. Maybe yesterday."

"Does he think there are other Burmese patrols in the area?" McShane asked.

Chan quickly relayed the question. Tah's expression was grave and his answer came in a rush of words. Chan hurriedly translated. "When these soldiers no come back, many more soldier come looking for them."

The team turned and looked at one another. Here we go again, McShane thought. Slowly, they were being drawn into a quagmire they had no business getting stuck in. This was supposed to be a simple get-in, get-out operation.

"Well guys," McShane said with a certain casualness, "I think we should be moving along. The last thing we want is to get caught in a dispute between the KNU and the Burmese."

"That's for sure," Pike added.

"Yeah, I know," Everett said. "You just want to get back to Bangkok so you can have a Big Mac."

"Got that right."

"All right, gentleman, just in case, let's have our weapons ready," McShane said. They moved off the side of the trail behind some boulders. For ease of storage, the team had broken down their CAR-15, fully automatic carbines into two pieces: the telescopic metal stock and the receiver group and barrel. They quickly re-attached the two halves, inserted a 30-round magazine, and positioned the weapons, barrel first into their rucks.

"Let's move it," McShane ordered.

They no longer felt they were on a leisurely hiking adventure. Chan had Tah pick up the pace considerably. He was now anxious to reach the safety of the village where they were to stay the night. Chan knew the Burmese army rarely attacked Karen villages unless there were known KNU hideouts, or they were provoked. He feared the attack by the KNU on the Burmese patrol was just such a provocation.

They arrived at the first KNU checkpoint shortly before sunset. The trail had narrowed considerably until it bottlenecked into an outcropping of massive boulders. Three soldiers appeared suddenly from behind the rocks and greeted Tah warmly. McShane scrutinized the rock formation, which he estimated to be at least a dozen meters tall. Scores of KNU soldiers, some dressed in fatigues, others in black shirts and loincloths, all carrying AK-47s, stared down on them curiously. McShane could see why the Burmese had never bothered the village. It would be impossible for them to get in, or out.

Chan leaned toward McShane. "This is Tah's village. These three men are his brothers. They take us to village now."

McShane nodded and signaled for the team to gather around. He studied each of their expressions. They looked hot and tired. He was sure they'd like the news. "Listen up. These men are Tah's brothers and they're taking us to their village. We'll stay there tonight."

"Thank God," Pike said. "I thought this day would never end."

They followed the narrow path for perhaps another quarter mile until it opened up into a bowl-shaped clearing. Scattered throughout the clearing, which McShane estimated to be at least a couple hundred meters in circumference, were dozens of huts elevated on bamboo poles. Rocky bluffs completely surrounded the village. KNU sentries stood guard along the top of the three and four story boulders. McShane marveled at the quirk of nature that allowed the Karen villagers to live hidden from civilization behind this shield of stone. He wondered how long the village had been here, and if the Burmese even knew of its existence.

They ventured in toward the center of the village. Children, as well as their elders, stopped whatever they were doing to gawk at the outsiders. McShane was pretty sure the villagers had never laid eyes on a white man. Makes sense, he decided. Until two days ago, he'd never seen a Karen.

The three brothers and Tah led the team to a longhouse at least twice the size of any of the huts. One of the brothers scrambled up the bamboo ladder/stairs and disappeared inside the longhouse. Soon, a stooped man with long, gray hair flowing down to his shoulders emerged from the bamboo building. Tah whispered something into Chan's ear.

Chan turned to McShane. "Old man is headman. He is eighty-year-old. Born this village. To him we are like celebrities." He thought for a moment then grinned, "Like Beatles. We stay his house."

McShane couldn't help but chuckle at Chan's comparing his team to The Beatles. But he understood Chan's point, and how significant their visit was. As soon as he had the opportunity, he'd brief the team on just how important their presence was, and to be on their best behavior. He'd definitely stress the subject of table manners to Pike. McShane estimated they were probably outgunned by fifty-to-one and he didn't want Pike's picky eating habits to piss anyone off.

The headman motioned the team to come up. After taking off their boots, they joined him inside. He sat cross-legged on the bamboo slat floor at the head of a long, split-teak log table. Each team member took a place at the table. Several women, who McShane guessed were his daughters, and perhaps granddaughters, handed each of them a bamboo cup filled with hot tea. McShane, seated directly across from Pike, glared at him to make sure he drank it. Pike winked back and slowly sipped from the cup.

The headman directed his attention toward Chan, who sat directly to his right, and began to speak. His voice was so soft that McShane could barely hear him. Chan replied several times with a simple nod. When the headman finished talking, he motioned toward one of the women and she hurried to his side. She helped him to his feet and led him through a door into another room.

Chan turned and faced the team. "Headman welcome us to village. We honor guests. Tah and brothers his great-grandsons. They tell him we here to kill many Burmese soldiers."

"Chan," McShane interrupted, "what makes him think that? We are supposed to be on a trekking trip. Nobody is supposed to know why we are here. And it is certainly not to kill Burmese."

"Tah tell him."

"Tah?" McShane was irritated. Why the hell would he think we were here to kill Burmese soldiers? McShane was beginning to wonder if Rayburn hadn't told Chan to tell Tah more than he was supposed to know. "How the hell should he know? He's just our guide."

Chan shrugged his shoulders and feigned stupidity. "He just know. Smart kid. Maybe see you take out gun."

McShane doubted that. The team had made damn sure they were well concealed before they had reassembled their CARs. Maybe Tah was a smart kid, but somehow he didn't think he was that damn smart. No, someone had told him. Maybe it was Rayburn or maybe Chan. Well, it was too late to worry about it now. The cat was definitely out of the bag and by now the entire village was in on their little secret. McShane more fully understood why they were celebrities, like The Beatles. The only difference was they were here to kill Burmese, not play music.

That night the villagers put on a great welcome party for the team. They slaughtered a pig and roasted it over a huge fire pit located at the center of the village. The team sat on log benches near the fire. Several curious Karen children crowded around to watch. McShane supposed they must look like giants to them. They were served teak bowls brimming with white pork, rice, and various vegetables. Several times, McShane glanced furtively at Pike. To his surprise, he ate as hungrily as the villagers.

Afterwards, several Karen men brought out long cylindrical instruments that resembled bassoons. They watched in amusement as the men performed a kind of shuffling dance around the pit, blowing into their bamboo bassoons. They played a repetitive tune that to McShane sounded as if consisted of only about three notes. Soon, it seemed the entire village was dancing around the fire.

One by one, each of the team members was coerced into dancing by one of the many young and single Karen women. They loved Pike, who hammed it up as much as he dared, imitating Michael Jackson's moon-walk. McShane was thankful the villagers hadn't served rice wine. Pike would have been a handful after a few drinks of that.

The music, dancing, and eating went well into the night. Eventually the villagers began drifting off to their huts until only the team, Chan, and a few elders remained standing.

"Must sleep," Chan said, as he yawned. "Leave early."

McShane had seen Chan earlier speaking to several KNU. He was curious as to what he may have learned.

"Chan, did you find out anything about the Burmese Army or the white man helping the KNU?"

Chan arched his back and stretched. "A little. Burmese Army increase attacks on KNU, but no get into this village. Village we go tomorrow attacked last week. That why KNU attack patrol yesterday. For revenge. Now they afraid of bigger attack. But many KNU come help. KNU from this village already there, and tomorrow many KNU go with us."

"What about the white man?"

"They see him before at the other village. He has Karen wife and two child. Nobody know where he come from. He speak only Karen language."

This bit of news stunned McShane. Would the Canadian or a hired mercenary have a family and speak Karen? He doubted it. The evidence now pointed away from the Canadian and mercenary hypothesis, and more towards someone else, like Kevin Slade. McShane's heart skipped a beat. He'd always figured the man in the photo was someone other than Slade, and hadn't entirely prepared himself to be wrong. It was too hard to believe. There must be another explanation, he convinced himself.

The next morning, after a breakfast of hard-boiled eggs, the team left the village by another trail that crossed over a narrow stream, and headed back into the rocks. Tah was in the lead, along with another five KNU. Trailing behind Evans who, as the weapons sergeant, was usually the team's tail gunner, were an additional half dozen soldiers. They were well-armed with AK-47s, including an RPD. McShane felt more secure than he had since their departure the previous morning. If they did encounter any resistance from the Burmese Army, they'd be able to put up a hell of a fight.

Once they exited the craggy rock formation, the terrain varied little from the day before. As they ascended the mountain, McShane got a good look at the valley below. The early morning sun glistened off the dingy water on tiny plots of terraced, green rice paddies. He made out several water buffalo pulling wooden ploughs through the muck. Stooped villagers toiled in the paddies, planting rice seedlings. A few young men stood nearby, next to a wagon draped with a tarp. McShane guessed they were KNU guarding the villagers and that beneath the tarp were their weapons. He wondered why the Burmese Army didn't bomb the fields, knowing they provided food for the KNU. He reminded himself to ask Chan later.

As they rounded a sharp bend in the trail, McShane thought he heard automatic weapons fire in the distance. In the thick jungle foliage, it was impossible to determine how far away the gun shots were. They could be just a few hundred meters ahead, or echoing up the valley from several miles away. Suddenly, the KNU soldiers in front of him increased their pace to a trot.

-CHAPTER TWELVE-

SLADE HUNKERED DOWN BEHIND a tree stump and directed his attention toward the dusty trail thirty meters to his right front. Pru took up position a few feet away behind a man-sized fern and aimed the RPD down the trail. The other KNU guerillas were hidden in the dense brush to Slade's left and right. They waited patiently for the Burmese Army patrol to approach.

Slade had underestimated the tenacity of the Burmese Army. Once they learned their patrol had been ambushed, another patrol in the immediate vicinity had taken up pursuit. They had been relentless. The morning after the ambush, Slade had led the squad away from the cave toward their village, only to be cut off by another Burmese patrol. He and his force of KNU guerillas had been trying to outwit and outmaneuver the Burmese ever since. Additional Burmese reinforcements had come and were tracking them. Up until now, because of their smaller size and jungle experience, he and his KNU had managed to stay out of their grasp.

The day was miserably hot and Slade wiped a bead of perspiration from his brow. He was growing weary of being constantly on the move, trying to keep the Burmese at bay. But the enemy's stamina and persistence had been unwavering. The fat man they killed in the ambush must have been very important for the Burmese to commit so much manpower to hunting them down. He wished he'd paid more attention in the cave when Shan tried to tell him about the documents on the man's body. They probably held the key. But, they'd been on the run since shortly after leaving the cave complex and he hadn't had the opportunity to question Shan about the documents.

They were only a few klicks from their jungle camp, but Slade wanted to make damn certain the Burmese were off their backs before they continued on. He didn't want to risk leading them there. He'd considered laying low for a day or two, rather than ambushing another patrol. Perhaps the Burmese would lose patience, and leave the area. Once the soldiers left, they could return to the village without being followed.

Suddenly, his heartbeat accelerated. The point element of a Burmese Army patrol rounded the sharp bend in the trail and headed toward their kill zone. As soon as the main body of the patrol entered the kill zone, Pru was to initiate the ambush by opening fire with his RPD machine gun. But after what he'd just considered, he didn't think it was a wise move. He turned to tell Pru to hold his fire when he was confronted with the worst possible scenario.

An overanxious Karen to his right prematurely opened up on the two-man point team. There was no turning back, now. In unison, everyone but Slade opened up on the soldiers. Under such intense gunfire, their bodies exploded in a crimson mist.

Slade shook his head. He was disappointed in the lapse of discipline. Up until this moment, the KNU soldiers under his command had always performed professionally, particularly when conducting an ambush. That was their specialty: hit and run. They'd practiced various ambush techniques dozens of times and initiated them at least a dozen times in the past year.

Well, it was too late to worry about it now, he told himself. By now, he surmised, the main force of Burmese soldiers had been alerted and taken up a defensive posture. Shortly, they'd regroup and begin to flank their position. Their only course of action was to pick up and, once again, run for their lives.

Shan shouted to his men to fall back. At a dead run the guerillas followed him up the steep mountain slope. Slade and Pru hung back a moment longer. They would hold off the Burmese for a while if they came their way. They waited what seemed a millennium, but in reality amounted to less than a couple of minutes. Slade kept his ear tuned to the jungle. It was deathly silent. He wondered if the Burmese had turned and run, or were just biding their time. He'd wait a minute or two longer.

Just as he was about to signal Pru to fall back, a group of four soldiers slowly rounded the bend. They eyed the trail cautiously as they approached the remains of their two fallen comrades. One of the soldiers knelt down on one knee next to the bodies, while the others kept a wary lookout. The soldier unclasped a radio handset from his ammunition belt. Slade noted the radio strapped to his back was a Vietnam era PRC-25.

The soldier shouted into the handset. The others momentarily dropped their guard and turned toward him. Slade glanced over at Pru. He was caressing the trigger of the RPD with his forefinger. Slade knew he wanted to open fire. That's what the KNU lived for, killing Burmese. He thought about whether they should kill the soldiers.

Slade reached over and tapped Pru on the shoulder. Pru grinned devilishly. Slade knew at that instant he couldn't hold him back. So he nodded to the young guerilla and together they opened fire. The soldiers went down immediately. Slade had to grab Pru by the shoulder to get him to quit firing. He yanked him to his knees and they hastily followed the route the others had taken a few minutes earlier.

Thick jungle foliage clawed at their loose, black clothing as they moved up the slope. The lugged soles of the KNU's boots had churned up the earth, making their trail easy to follow. Slade hoped the remaining Burmese soldiers were frightened and confused enough not to search for them. He doubted they would. He had learned over the years that the Burmese Army traveled only on established roads and trails. Rarely did they venture off the beaten path. The Karen, however, had lived in the heavily forested jungles of southern Burma for centuries and knew ways the Burmese would never think of to get around the inhospitable jungle.

The air was horrendously hot and muggy. Slade and Pru took frequent breaks to rest and listen for signs they were being followed. Slade was sure what was left of the patrol had retreated. However, nightfall was still several hours away, and there was always a chance they'd encounter one of the other patrols. They'd have to be vigilant.

An hour later they caught up to the others. They had taken refuge in a thicket of dense scrub. A guard posted near the trees led them into the interior of the thicket. The guerillas sat around in a small clearing within the heavy pocket of undergrowth, drinking water. Slade sat next to Shan and pulled out his canteen. The water was tepid and tasted musty. But after so many years of living in the mountainous hill tribe regions of Southeast Asia, he'd grown accustomed to the taste. He closed his eyes and leaned back against a tree trunk.

He was anxious to return to their camp. They had been out so long, harassing Burmese Army patrols, that he sorely missed his wife, Soon, and Mar, their daughter. He hoped they could make it back in time. He wanted to scoop them up and hug them and never let go.

On three different occasions, when Mar had become ill, they'd sneaked across the border into Thailand to seek medical treatment at the hospital in Mae Hong Son. The hospital was known for treating wounded KNU soldiers and refugees caught up in the war. A horrific injury common to many of the Karen was leg amputations caused by Burmese land mines. Nearly a quarter of the patients in the Mae Hong Son hospital suffered from some form of amputation. Once at the hospital, he witnessed an American doctor demonstrate to the Thai medical staff a procedure for implanting a titanium rod into the stump of an anesthetized male. Hinged to the bottom of the rod was a plate, roughly the shape of a foot. It was crude, but an affective, inexpensive prostheses.

There was a time when he had tried to convince his wife to move to Thailand. They could live in one of the many mountain villages, he'd explained. Far enough from civilization to live peacefully without fear of reprisals by the Burmese Army, yet close enough to a town where they could obtain basic comforts. Mar could go to school, maybe become a doctor and help her own people. But Soon would have none of it. She was born in the mountains of Burma, and that was where she would die. To her, it was unthinkable to consider giving up their cause. Her father had fought against the tyrannical Burmese government, as had two of her brothers. All three were murdered in a single afternoon when she was twelve, by soldiers who attacked their village. From that day forth, she swore she'd live to see the day when the Karen would have their own land, their own government.

He'd never suggested moving again. But the events of the past few weeks had caused him to reconsider. The Burmese seemed hell bent on either beating the Karen into total submission or eradicating them from Burma altogether. Sure, the KNU had managed to harass the Burmese and inflict casualties. But the tradeoff in Karen suffering was too high. There was no end in sight, and he was tired. For over twenty years he'd been involved in someone else's fight and his only desire now was to live his final years in peace.

He found himself thinking about his life before he'd joined the army in 1965. He tried to conjure an image of his parents, who'd both been killed in a traffic accident on California's Pacific Coast Highway outside the seaside town of Bolinas, north of San Francisco. They'd gone for the weekend, leaving him and his brother, Paul, with an aunt in the Pacific Heights area of San Francisco. He was fourteen, his brother eleven.

His Aunt Virginia raised them. He went to Balboa High School in the city, lettered in varsity football and track. A mediocre student, he decided not to go on to college when an Army recruiter visited the school in the last month of his senior year and talked several of his football teammates into enlisting. Vietnam wasn't a household name yet, but he wanted to be part of it.

Well, he'd certainly gotten his share of Vietnam, he reflected, and then some. A week after graduating, he was in basic training at Fort Ord, California. From there he went to advanced infantry in Louisiana then on to airborne training in Georgia and finally volunteered for Special Forces in North Carolina. It was all such a blur now. So much had happened since then that he had a hard time recalling any of it. Sometimes he wondered if any of it had really happened.

He often wondered what had become of his old team. Did Broderick, Mullins, and Lofton make it out safely? Were they married? Children? He hoped so, and that they were successful. What he'd done by staying in Southeast Asia, not returning to his own country after the war, he knew, was a cop out of sorts. He was afraid of facing a society that had displayed such indifference through most of the war, a society that couldn't have cared less about the sacrifices he and hundreds of thousands of others had made. A society that had forgotten their sacrifices. At the time, he felt his duty was to help people who cared. He found those people in the mountains of Laos and Burma.

Shan came over and sat next to him. "My brother, you look tired. What have you been thinking?"

Slade opened his eyes, and rubbed them with the palm of his dirt-smeared hands. "I *am* tired, Shan. I have been thinking of Soon and Mar. I do not want them to live in constant fear, anymore. I wish I could talk her into moving to a resettlement camp in the mountains of Thailand, safe from the bloodshed. But I know that is impossible. She will never leave Burma."

Shan studied the American carefully. They had been friends for nearly fourteen years. As a Karen, he had left Burma in 1968 to escape persecution. He resettled in the Thai/Lao border town of Nakhon Phanom, hearing that Americans were hiring mercenaries to help fight the communists in Laos. For three years, he worked for the American Green Berets. After the war in Vietnam was over, he was again employed by the Americans, this time to look for missing American soldiers in Laos.

One day, when he was returning from the Royal Thai Air Force base where the Green Berets launched their missions into Laos, he saw an American walking along the road dressed in faded jungle fatigue pants and a white Singha beer T-shirt. At the time, he thought he was one of the Americans from the Green Beret camp located outside Nakhon Phanom. He gave the man, who said his name was Slade, a ride on his Honda 50 to the small house he shared with two other Karen working for the Americans. Slade had been too tired to speak and slept for two days on a mat next to his own. On the third day, after eating three bowls of rice and dried fish, he explained that he wasn't a soldier, but a tourist who had become lost in the jungle.

Shan never believed him, but kept his thoughts to himself, never questioning him about his past. Slade lived at the house with them for two months, teaching English at the local Thai high school. When the Americans closed their base at the airfield in Nakhon Phanom, he asked Slade if he wanted to go with him to Burma to see his family. Slade agreed, and it wasn't until that long trek to his mountain village that he learned the truth about the American.

At the time, he had felt sorry for Slade and all that he'd gone through. No man, he thought, should suffer so much in one lifetime. He introduced him to his younger sister, Soon, who was eighteen, ripe for marriage. Slade lived in the same house with Shan, Soon, and their mother for three months. After that, Shan helped Slade build a house of his own and shortly afterwards, Slade asked Soon to marry him.

Soon and Slade lived a life of contentment for several months. One day when Shan and Slade were out hunting, a Burmese Army patrol came into their village. The soldiers demanded rice and meat. When the headman refused, the soldiers beat him and his wife with their rifle butts. They took the rice they'd harvested for the winter and six pigs. The next week when a KNU recruiter came to their village, they readily agreed to join in the fight for freedom. He and Slade were given the task of training all the new recruits in the area, which consisted of more than a hundred men in four villages.

They had fought the Burmese ever since, forced to move their village every few years to avoid harassment. Yes, he, too, was tired. Tired of fighting, tired of moving. He and Slade were both approaching their middle years and should be living a life of relaxation, like their forefathers. He had often thought of settling in Thailand. They could still carry on the fight from there.

"Maybe I could talk my sister into moving to Thailand, Slade. We could all go, start a new village on the other side of the border."

"I would like that, Shan. But, you know how your sister feels about leaving Burma. She feels she would be letting her people down, deserting them."

"Yes, I know. That is why I say move the whole village across the border. We could still go into Burma and fight." He rested a hand on Slade's shoulder. "I will talk to her when we get back."

"Well, you can try." Slade settled back against the tree trunk and closed his eyes again. He sighed softly and whispered. "She can only say no."

Shan nodded and watched as his friend dozed off. He was right, she could only say no, but he had a strong feeling that he could convince her this time. First, however, they had to get back to the village safely. He wished he could let Slade sleep for a few minutes, but knew they couldn't risk staying in one place for too long.

He lightly squeezed Slade's shoulder, waking him with a start.

"We must go, brother."

- CHAPTER THIRTEEN -

THE MACHINE GUN BURST lasted only for a few seconds, but was quickly followed by a much longer one, accompanied by several small weapons firing full automatic. To McShane, the weapons fire sounded very near. The KNU soldiers abruptly stepped up their pace and were soon at a dead run. Sandwiched between the two KNU guerilla elements, the team didn't have much of a choice but to keep up. McShane prayed they weren't on a collision course with a pissed-off Burmese Army unit.

Without warning, the KNU soldier McShane followed came to an abrupt halt. He nearly slammed into the young soldier. Grunts and the rattle of equipment to the rear suggested that some of the others hadn't been as fortunate. He turned and checked on his team. Everyone was still standing, only a little out of breath. His attention was redirected forward when the KNU point element suddenly opened fire. McShane swore and dived into the brush, taking cover behind some low lying rocks.

McShane raised his head and peered over the rocks. He could see that the rest of the team had all taken cover and had their weapons trained on the path. Lieutenant Hansen lie next to him. Chan, he was pleased to notice, had found cover also. McShane checked the trail. The rear element of KNU had joined their comrades. There was some sporadic gunfire, but then it stopped. An eerie silence fell over the jungle.

Figuring they were out of immediate danger, McShane signaled the team onto the trail. They kept their CARs at the ready. Several meters away a group of KNU huddled at the edge of the trail. They spoke animatedly to a wounded Burmese soldier. He motioned Chan forward.

"Can you tell what they are saying, Chan?" McShane asked.

"They talk to wounded Burma soldier. But I cannot tell what they say."

The team huddled around Hansen and McShane. "Stay alert," McShane cautioned. "The Burmese may be just around the corner. Let's check out what the commotion is about."

As the team approached the KNU soldiers, they saw several dead Burmese scattered on the hillside and trail. McShane counted at least eight. The KNU guerrillas were already scavenging their bodies for weapons, ammo, grenades, and useful clothing items. Some of the KNU tried on the dead soldiers' boots, a highly cherished piece of equipment. It was impossible to determine how many wounded escaped the slaughter, but McShane noticed several blood trails leading away from the path.

They joined the cluster of soldiers. One of the KNU soldiers straddled the wounded Burmese. The soldier had his arms pinned to the ground with his knees. The Burmese soldier's eyes were wide with fear. The KNU had the small blade of his Swiss Army pocket knife inserted into the Burmese's right nostril. McShane was angry. He knew what the Karen guerrilla was about to do. He'd not come to Burma to be a party to torture. He stepped forward and grabbed the Karen's wrist. The team tensed, fearing the possible ramifications of his interference.

McShane's actions happened so quickly that Chan didn't have time to react. While he understood why McShane did what he did, the American did not fully understand that the Karen had suffered horrific persecution under the Burmese for generations. Chan only hoped that the KNU wouldn't be too offended, or the Americans may find themselves fighting the very people they came to help.

McShane pulled the knife away from the soldier's nose. He smiled at the Karen soldier, snapped the blade closed, and handed it back to him. McShane didn't care whether the Karen or the others were angry or not. He wasn't going to tolerate any misconduct, even if this war wasn't his business. He just couldn't allow it while he was present. Surprisingly, the Karen soldier smiled back at McShane and returned the knife to his pants pocket.

"Payne, get up here and see what you can do for this soldier."

Travis Payne pulled the aid bag from his rucksack and knelt down beside the Burmese. Blood poured from his shoulder and stomach. The abdominal wound was life threatening. The only way the soldier was going to make it, Payne knew, was if the Burmese could get to a hospital. And Payne knew that was highly unlikely. He quickly injected the soldier with a Blistex sized-tube syrette of morphine. Besides stemming the flow of blood and binding the wounds, it was about all he could do.

"Mr. McShane," Chan said, grinning. "That was very dangerous. You are lucky. I think the Karen soldier is afraid of you."

"Tell him and the others that we need the soldier alive. He can tell us where the other Burmese soldiers are located. Tell them he is hurt very badly, and if he is hurt any more he will die. If we keep him alive, and he tells us where to find the others, then the KNU can achieve a great victory."

Chan's grin broadened. He liked this American more and more every day. Besides, Chan thought to himself, he was right. The soldier was more valuable to them alive and well. If they showed him some kindness, he was more likely to tell them what they wanted to know. He turned to the KNU guerrillas and in his best Karen explained to them why the American had not wanted them to harm the enemy soldier. The soldiers nodded and without being told, took up defensive positions along the trail.

"What do you think, Travis?" McShane said as he crouched next to Payne. The team's medic had the soldier's shirt spread open. There was a puncture wound the size of his thumb a couple inches above his navel. "Is he going to make it?"

Payne shook his head. "Not if he doesn't get to a hospital soon. And we know that's not going to happen. He lost a lot of blood while that KNU was fucking with him. All I can do is clean the wound and dress it. Already gave him a shot of morphine to relax him.

Right now he's high as a kite. I'll give him another one after he's bandaged."

"Maybe now's the time to interrogate him." McShane suggested. "He might be so stoned that he'll tell us everything we want to know."

"Good possibility."

McShane stood. "I'll get Chan to ask him where their camp is. Then we've got to move on. We've already lost valuable daylight fartin' around here. And now that we have to carry the soldier, we'll be hard pressed to make it to the village tonight. The KNU can hit the Burmese camp tomorrow or the next day."

Payne gently wiped blood from around the entry wound with a 6x6 gauze bandage soaked in Betadine. The soldier moaned softly. Payne knew it was fruitless. The exit wound in his lower back was the size of his fist. On top of that, he was pretty sure the bullet had severed his spinal cord. At best, if he survived, he would be paralyzed from the waist down. He didn't want to turn him onto his side so he could dress the exit until Chan questioned him. The shock of moving him would likely kill him.

"Chan," McShane said, "ask him where their camp is."

Chan knew little Burmese, but figured Tah spoke and understood enough to ask the questions. He found him crouched next to a tree growing out of the embankment at an odd, forty-five degree angle. He motioned him over.

Chan's Karen was not the best, but after taking tourists on hill tribe treks for more than ten years, he managed.

"Tah, ask soldier where his camp is."

Tah squatted next to the soldier and looked him over. The American medic was tying a battle dressing over the wound in his stomach. Tah suddenly felt remorse for the Burmese soldier. He was even younger than himself, looking more like a boy than a soldier. He wondered if the soldier truly understood why he was fighting against the KNU. He doubted it. His superiors had probably told him and his comrades many lies so they would fight.

"Where is your camp, my friend," Tah whispered in his ear. The soldier moaned softly. His eyes, vacant and glazed, stared fixedly up at the trees. To Tah, there seemed to be little life left in them. He wouldn't live much longer, he knew.

"Please, tell me where your camp is located so that we can take you there." The soldier uttered something and Tah pressed his ear close to his mouth, but couldn't make out his words. He pulled his head back and looked at the soldier again. His eyes were now closed. Tah looked over at the American who shook his head. Tah knew the soldier was with his ancestors now.

"That it, Travis?" McShane asked.

"Yep, that's it. Save us a lot of trouble, that's for sure. What do you want to do with him?"

"Just leave him with the others," McShane said matter-of-factly. "I don't know what the Burmese Army's policy is for policing their dead, but I imagine they don't bother with 'em. Not our concern, anyway. Pack your aid bag. We're outta here. We've wasted enough time."

Payne wasn't about to argue with his team sergeant. He felt uneasy, certain the Burmese would return at any moment. He hastily crammed the Betadine, unused bandages, and empty syrette back into his bag and then stood. McShane and Lieutenant Hansen had already taken up positions behind the KNU point element. Payne fell in behind Hansen with Chan, Everett, Pike, and Evans following him. He couldn't get away from the Burmese dead quick enough.

They continued down the trail at a slower pace than before, although the KNU still traveled at a clip that was too fast for McShane. With so many Burmese in the area, he would have moved much more cautiously. In fact, he never would have used the trail, using the jungle for cover instead. If his team ever got around to training the KNU, he would definitely have them work on their patrolling techniques. He just prayed the Burmese were gone.

An hour later, they turned off the trail and cut through the jungle. McShane heard running water. A few minutes later they stood before a rock precipice enclosed in vines and dense foliage. A small sliver of water poured from a crevice within the rocks and emptied into a clear pool at the base of the craggy cliff. One by one, the KNU knelt by the pond to fill their canteens. McShane glanced around nervously. He wondered if the Burmese knew about the watering hole.

The KNU who'd been traveling behind the team formed a tight defensive perimeter around them, reassuring McShane. He crouched and filled two of his canteens. In turn, the team members topped off their canteens. McShane cupped his hands and dipped them into the pool. The water was cool and clear. He splashed his face with the refreshing liquid, allowing the water to run down his neck and onto his shirt. The sound of the splattering water soothed McShane's frayed nerves. He almost felt human again.

Once the point element had replenished their water, the others came forward. The point element then took over the task of providing security. McShane and the team took advantage of the brief respite and sat on the roots of a mammoth banyan tree.

"Looks like a picture from a travel magazine," Colin Evans remarked.

"How the hell would you know? Weapons men don't read," Pike kidded.

"Yeah, but we look at the pictures." Evans replied, smiling.

McShane was about to make another dig at his weapons man when he noticed a flicker of movement several meters into the jungle. He studied the foliage intently. He quickly looked around. As far as he could tell, all the KNU were present. His heart skipped a beat. What he had feared most the past hour was now reality.

"I think we have visitors, guys," McShane whispered. "Look to my right, about twenty meters into the jungle."

All eyes focused on the spot where McShane had seen the movement. Several crouched forms were slowly making their way toward them. Nearly simultaneously, the team flicked the selector switches on their CARs one click, from safe to auto.

"Chan," McShane said in a barely audible whisper.

Chan sat on a round rock by the pool talking to Tah. He turned toward McShane. The American pointed in the direction of the jungle. Chan squinted and peered into the depths of the thick foliage. His mouth opened as if he was about to say something. He grabbed Tah's wrist to get his attention.

"Tah," he said in hushed tones. "Look."

Tah had already seen the Burmese and reacted instantly. He turned to two KNU sitting next to them. They, too, sensed something was wrong and raised their weapons. The other KNU took cover behind rocks and trees. By now, McShane's team was in position behind some rocks, waiting for the Burmese Army patrol to make their next move. So much for peace and quiet, McShane thought. He aligned his front sight post on the chest of a soldier fifteen meters away.

McShane counted at least a dozen Burmese soldiers through the jungle thicket. They advanced slowly, taking a step, then stopping and listening, then continuing, much the same way his old team used to travel in Laos. They seemed unaware of the team's presence. He couldn't believe they hadn't been seen. Well, at least they had the element of surprise. He tightened his hold on his weapon and took a deep breath.

A noise behind McShane startled him. He swung around. One of the KNU guerrillas was bending over to pick up his AK-47. Apparently he had dropped it. McShane swore to himself and spun back around. The Burmese had frozen in place.

The soldiers remained as motionless as Greek statues. They were such an easy target that McShane wondered if they shouldn't open up on them now. He blinked away a bead of sweat that had trickled from his forehead and prepared for the worst. It didn't take long for the stalemate to end.

Suddenly, the silence was broken when, without warning, the KNU opened fire. It was a vicious and intense fusillade of automatic weapons fire. Rounds snapped terrifyingly overhead. The noise in the enclosed space was ear-shattering. McShane and the team hunkered down and joined in the onslaught.

Exposed and with few places to take cover, the Burmese had little chance for survival. One by one, the soldiers were struck down. McShane doubted if a single soldier got off a shot. Then, as abruptly as it had started, the gunfire ceased. A haze of cordite smoke hung over the jungle like Los Angeles smog. It was impossible to see clearly. McShane sucked in a breath of the acrid smoke and squinted his eyes.

Before he could determine if anyone was still standing, the KNU were already moving into the jungle. The guerrillas quickly swarmed over the Burmese positions. The team stood.

"Damn, that was *intense*," Pike remarked.

"Yeah!" Payne added. "It'd be a fucking miracle if anyone survived that shit."

McShane started to move forward. "Let's check it out."

The team found a grizzly sight. Strewn over the jungle duff were the remains of fifteen Burmese soldiers. Their bodies had literally been torn to shreds during the mad minute of gunfire. Limbs had been severed from torsos, eyes plucked from sockets, ears ripped from heads, and faces disfigured beyond recognition.

McShane resisted looking at the bodies directly. The sight of them sickened him. Over the years, he'd been exposed to death countless times. Yet still, he'd never grown accustomed to it. What bothered him was that he'd held no animosity toward the Burmese. He and his team were in Burma solely to prove or disprove the existence of an American MIA. Never had he imagined that he would be killing, once again.

As he passed among the dead, one of the bodies caught his attention. He thought he detected signs of life. Kneeling alongside the soldier, he studied him carefully. A sudden breeze scattered dry leaves and swirled smoke through the jungle, causing him to look up. Had he heard something off to his right, he wondered, or was it simply the sound of tree branches scraping together? He was about to turn his attention back to the soldier when he noticed the distinct sound again. It wasn't tree branches, he now concluded. He quickly stood and raised his CAR to his shoulder. And then it began again.

McShane fired half a magazine at two Burmese soldiers who'd suddenly emerged from the brush with six others. From what McShane could determine, his group was being attacked from three fronts. This time they were on the receiving end of the gunfire and he didn't like it. Burmese soldiers assaulted from everywhere. Emptying the remainder of the magazine at the Burmese, his only thought was to get his team safely out. He recalled the animal track he'd seen earlier behind the falls.

Pike and Payne were to his immediate right, squeezing off rounds. Hansen and Everett stood behind and to the left, spraying the underbrush with measured, automatic fire. He couldn't see Evans.

"Pull back to the waterfall," McShane yelled above the din of gunfire.

They fired off one last burst, turned, and retreated toward the falls. McShane wasn't worried about the KNU. They could take care of themselves. His concern was for his team. They were his family and he alone was responsible for their survival.

The firefight continued as the team regrouped behind a mound of rocks at the base of the cliffs. Miraculously, nobody had been hit. The team kept their eyes on the KNU. They held their ground, taking cover behind the fallen soldiers from the first attack. They were a courageous bunch, McShane thought, not yielding an inch to the Burmese assault. McShane saw a couple KNU go down and he experienced a moment of sadness at the loss of such brave men.

"We'll wait for the KNU a moment more," McShane said, out of breath. "Though, I'm afraid they'll stay and fight to the death." He glanced around. "Anyone see Chan?"

"Not since the first firefight," Payne replied.

"Shit. We can't leave without him." McShane scanned the pool area and the outcropping of rocks where he'd last seen Chan sitting with Tah. His gaze settled on a crumpled form behind a rock. He realized immediately from the white T-shirt that it was Chan. "Damn, there he is. Let's pull him back into the rocks."

Everett and Evans rushed forward. Each grabbed one of Chan's arms, and pulled him behind the rocks. McShane crouched next to Chan and rolled him onto his back. Blood oozed from a bullet hole in his neck. Payne felt for a pulse then shook his head.

"He's gone, Steve."

"Goddammit," McShane muttered. "None of this shit was supposed to happen."

Payne rested his hand on his team leader's shoulder. He knew how fond McShane had grown of the wiry little Thai. "You *know*, shit happens."

"Yeah, I know. But not like this. He wasn't a soldier, just a damn tour guide."

McShane's attention was drawn back to the firefight. The KNU were losing ground to an obviously superior Burmese force. They had lost half their men. He realized they had to go back and help before they were all slaughtered.

"Let's give 'em a hand," McShane ordered.

The team flanked to the left of the remaining KNU and advanced on the Burmese from their blind side. Tossing grenades and firing full-auto, they caught the Burmese off guard. They abruptly ceased firing and fled into the jungle.

"Pull back," McShane hollered, motioning the KNU back toward the waterfall. Without hesitation, they obeyed his order, dragging their dead with them.

The KNU followed McShane and the team to the animal track that skirted the craggy cliffs. All of the KNU had been wounded at least once, but still had the strength to carry one of their dead. Evans carried Chan over his shoulder. McShane knew they wouldn't be able to carry the bodies much farther. He began scanning the jungle foliage for a suitable place to dump the bodies. The KNU, he thought, could return later to recover the remains.

A hundred meters from the falls, he noticed a pile of deadfall a few meters off the trail. It was about the size of the English Thames van he had in high school and figured it was large enough to conceal all the bodies. He led them to the deadfall.

"Colin," McShane said out of breath, "dump Chan here. Hopefully, the KNU will get the picture and unload their dead also."

But the KNU didn't get it. Instead, they just stood in a semi-circle around the brush, watching curiously as Evans covered Chan's body with deadfall. McShane even tried using sign language, but they simply stared at him blankly. Then he thought about Everett, who knew something of the Thai language. Perhaps he could explain to Tah.

"Colin, how much Thai do you remember?"

Everett shrugged. "I don't know, why?"

"Tell Tah to dump the bodies. They can come back later and pick 'em up. Tell him to hurry."

"I'll give it try." Everett thought for a moment, trying to recall the necessary vocabulary. Then he turned and faced Tah, pointing to the brush. He spoke slowly and deliberately. "Tah, put dead here," he said in halting Thai. "Come back tomorrow." He waved his arm in the direction of the waterfall. "Burmese come. We hurry now."

Tah said something to the KNU and to Everett's surprise they laid the bodies next to Chan's and covered them up.

Everett beamed. "I'll be damned."

"Good job," McShane commended. "Now, let's get out of here."

As they returned to the trail everyone's attention was suddenly drawn in the direction of the waterfall. Gunfire had resumed. McShane was puzzled. Who were the Burmese fighting, now, he asked himself? Maybe it was time for Everett to break radio silence and call in the other half of the team along with an exfil chopper? This wasn't part of his job description.

-CHAPTER FOURTEEN-

SLADE AND THE KNU had only been on the go for an hour when they heard the rapid-fire sounds of automatic weapons. From the intensity of the firefight, Slade surmised dozens of weapons were involved. The patrol pulled off to the side of the trail and listened. Gunshots rang out for several seconds then tapered off, only to increase again. This time the sharp report of a half-dozen detonating grenades added to the mix. Slade wondered what other KNU unit could possibly be in the area.

He altered their direction of travel away from the camp and toward the gunfire. Hopefully, they could intervene in time to help. But he was still baffled. He didn't know of any other KNU unit operating in the area.

Even more perplexing was an unmistakable sound he hadn't heard in years, not since Vietnam. The KNU carried whatever weapons they could scrounge, either Chinese manufactured AK-47s, SKSs, and occasionally some Vietnam era M-16s. But the sound he heard was that of a CAR-15, the fully automatic, shortened version of the M-16 that many US Special Forces carried into Laos and Cambodia. Unless the Burmese army was issuing CARs to their troops, the only explanation was that a Thai Special Forces unit was operating in the area. Thai SF were the only troops in this part of the world outfitted with the weapon. His curiosity was definitely aroused.

As they cut through a thickly forested area, the firefight abruptly ended and once again the jungle grew silent. But Slade wasn't about to turn back just because the shooting had ceased. He had to get to the bottom of the mystery and find out who was using the CARs. Was Thailand secretly confronting Burmese troops with Thai SF teams? Thailand was now governed by an ex-general, so anything was possible.

Shan was walking point several meters ahead of him. The remainder of the squad were spread out at five-meter intervals behind him. Shan, he felt, was traveling too fast for the type of terrain they were in. The squad was finding it impossible to avoid the dry limbs that cracked like thunder when disturbed by their lug-soled boots. Everything he'd taught them over the years about noise discipline, it seemed, had been tossed aside. He grew increasingly afraid Shan might lead them directly into the enemy's gun sights.

Suddenly, Shan came to an abrupt halt, listened for an instant, then signaled the squad to move into a thicket of scrub brush. Slade wondered what he'd heard or seen. He took cover behind the thick brush next to Shan.

"What did you see?" Slade asked him.

"Burmese soldier, maybe fifteen meters through trees."

"Do you think they heard us?" Slade asked, his voice barely a whisper.

Shan held his finger to his lips. "Shhhh. They are almost here."

A few moments later, Slade made out the forms of several Burmese soldiers through the brush. Many were wounded. One soldier, he noticed, was supporting a bloodied left arm with his right hand. Another was limping, a bright splotch of blood on his upper thigh. The soldiers were wide-eyed, dazed. Slade estimated no more than a dozen soldiers. The listless troops would be an easy target for his squad.

Shan must have been reading his mind, because he turned to him and held up his right hand. It was folded into the shape of a gun. He was grinning. He pulled his thumb back then snapped it forward, like the hammer on a pistol. Slade nodded and repeated the signal to the KNU next to him. In an instant, the motion was passed down the line of KNU. Slade turned back to follow the soldier's progress. They weren't more than ten meters from their position, now. The entire squad's attention was focused on Shan. When he fired, they'd all fire.

Shan made his move when one of the Burmese soldiers suddenly fixed his gaze on the brush where they lie hidden. Before the soldier could fully process what he was seeing, Shan leapt to his feet, firing. The squad followed the cue and was up and shooting a split second later.

Slade didn't have the heart to kill any of the wounded Burmese, and left that act to the guerrillas. In fact, he didn't have the heart to kill anyone anymore. He simply went through the motions, firing wildly, hoping it was someone else's bullet that actually did the killing. The KNU had no problem with that.

It was over as quickly as it had begun. Scattered about the forest were at least a score of dead and dying Burmese Army soldiers. Slade turned away from the carnage. Intermittent gunshots rang out. The KNU walked among the Burmese, firing a single bullet into the heads of those showing any signs of life. Slade ached for it to be over and hoped this was the last of the killing before they reached the tranquility of their camp.

Each of the KNU collected one of the soldier's weapons and ammunition pouches. Over the last couple days they had managed to confiscate thirty-five weapons: fifteen hidden in the cave from the ambush the day before and the twenty today. In addition, there were easily a thousand rounds or more in all the ammo pouches.

By the time they left the scene, the soldiers had been stripped of their fatigue shirts and boots. Those that missed out on the previous ambush made up for it. The guerrillas' own uniforms were a hodgepodge of traditional Karen black pajama-like pants and green Burmese fatigue shirts. After today's ambush, Slade noticed they now all had matching Burmese Army issue, lug-soled boots. Some even had an extra pair laced to the back of their issue rucksacks. A victorious day, he mused.

Even though they had encountered the soldiers likely involved in the earlier firefight, Slade's curiosity wasn't satisfied. There had been no CAR-15s on any of the bodies, confirming another unit, and not the Burmese, were firing the weapons. Something compelled him to find the source of the Vietnam War-era automatic carbine.

He directed Shan to retrace the soldiers' route by following their blood trails through the forest. Ten minutes later they heard the sound of running water. Slade thought he knew where he was now. He recalled a small waterfall he and Soon had visited a couple of times on their trips to Naisoi. On their last trip together, three years before, they had spent an entire afternoon by the clear pool, first bathing in the chilled water and later, after drying in the hot sun, making love. Regardless if it was the falls or not, it was running water, and he could wash the stench of bloodletting from his body.

Leery of taking the entire squad to investigate, in the event there might be more Burmese around, he and Shan traveled alone. They cautiously picked their way through the thick brush, trying to keep noise to a minimum. Pushing past a thick hedgerow, they came upon another grisly site. Thoughts of the waterfall vanished

Strewn among the trees, Slade guessed were another dozen dead Burmese. He figured this must be the location of the original firefight. He shifted his gaze from the bloodied face of a young Burmese soldier to the waterfall as it emptied frothy white waters into the emerald pool below. Yes, it was the waterfall where he and Soon had made love, but the memory was now replaced by images of mangled corpses. He felt a twinge of sadness at the loss of a beautiful memory. He longed to feel Soon in his arms again.

"Shan, go get the others," Slade said softly. "I'll wait here."

Shan nodded and quickly disappeared into the undergrowth. Slade wandered among the corpses toward the falls. He hoped to find some evidence that the weapons he had heard earlier were in fact CAR-15s. He kicked at the spent 7.62mm AK shell casings littering the ground, turning them over with the toe of his boot. Judging by all the brass, it was one hell of a firefight.

As he neared the pool, his attention was drawn to an outcropping of rocks. He knelt down and ran his fingers along the ground. What he saw caused his heart to accelerate. Mixed in with the AK shell casings were several smaller .223 caliber casings, the round used in the M-16 and CAR-15. He smiled. His suspicions had been confirmed. He continued his search. Behind a particularly high rock, large enough to provide cover for at least two individuals, he found scores of .223 casings on either side of the rock. Walking amidst the outcroppings, he discovered even more brass, some of it the AK's 7.62 and some of it .223.

Slade sat down on one of the rocks and stared at ripples of water spreading outward from the falls. He'd already formed a picture in his mind of what had likely happened at the falls fewer than twenty minutes before. A KNU unit had tangled with a Burmese patrol, he surmised. Among the KNU, he guessed, were a half-dozen other soldiers with either M-16s or CAR-15s. He suspected the latter, because the CAR's shorter barrel made a different sound.

He turned his attention away from the falls and studied the ground, wondering where the KNU and mystery soldiers had gone. His eyes locked on a wide streak of blood soaked into the dirt and duff that continued past the pool toward the cliffs. He stood and followed the blood trail as it meandered along a faint animal track paralleling the rock cliffs. Oddly, the ground was churned as though several people had passed.

Slade knelt when he noticed in the dust an imprint of a boot similar to the ones they got from the Burmese. But even more curious was the print of a boot a few feet away. He'd never seen one quite like it before. They were not Burmese or Thai jungle boots, which were merely cheap imitations of the old Vietnam style jungle boot. No, he thought, these looked like a type of civilian hiking boot that a tourist might buy at one of the large markets in Chiang Mai or Mae Hong Son. The strange boot sole impression only added to the mystery. He'd wait for the others and then they'd follow the animal track.

Shan showed up with the squad moments later. His men immediately began scavenging for additional equipment. Shan found Slade wandering near the cliffs, staring at the ground. He approached him slowly, afraid to disturb his thoughts.

"Shan, what do you think of these tracks?" Slade asked without looking up.

Shan turned his attention downward. At first, he didn't know what the American was asking him. To him, the earth looked as though it had been torn up by a wild pig routing for food. But upon closer inspection, he noticed dozens of boot marks. But he didn't understand the significance of the prints.

"I do not understand. They look like Burmese boots. Burmese come this way before the fight."

"Look more carefully. See, they are pointed in the opposite direction. The people wearing these boots were going away from the falls. And look here, these are not military." He pointed to a pair of prints with the tip of his AK muzzle.

"Yes, I see, but I do not know the meaning."

"I'm not sure either. Get the men. I want to follow the tracks. Maybe we'll find out what it means, and who fired on the Burmese soldiers."

Within moments, the squad rallied around Slade. Anxious to solve the mystery, he hastily led the KNU soldiers down the path. A couple hundred meters down the track, Slade noticed an opening in the dense jungle foliage. He stopped to look more closely. The underbrush, Slade noticed, had been trampled and some low-hanging tree limbs broken back. Several of the boot prints disappeared into the bushes.

"Shan, have the squad set up a perimeter. We'll go inside to look."

While Shan passed on the orders, Slade parted the underbrush and cautiously stepped inside the foliage. He proceeded slowly, the muzzle of his AK-47 moving with his eyes as he scanned the depths of the dark jungle. A few meters ahead his gaze locked on an unusual clump of deadfall. He thought he saw a hand sticking out from beneath the brush. He approached it wearily, his index finger caressing the trigger of his AK.

Shan soon joined him and together they began investigating the pile of undergrowth. Slade maneuvered to the rear of the deadfall. Suddenly, he stopped in his tracks, stunned by what he saw. Stacked behind the deadfall were the bloodied bodies of several men, some wearing Burmese fatigue shirts. As he moved nearer, he saw that most wore the baggy black pants of the Karen. Christ, he thought, they were KNU.

He glanced around nervously. It was awfully quiet. He half expected to see a platoon of Burmese soldiers bearing down on them. Quickly, he shrugged off his fears and approached Shan, who poked among the dead.

"I know this man," Shan said as he turned one of the bodies over. "He is married to Pru's cousin in a village near Doi Mae. He is very far from home. I wonder what he and these others were doing here?"

"I don't know, Shan. But they must have been the ones fighting the Burmese. It is obvious they were hidden here so their comrades could escape."

"Yes. They will come back when it is safe, and return the dead to their villages for burial."

The discovery of the bodies still didn't solve the mystery of who carried CAR-15s and wore civilian hiking boots. It was likely he'd never learn the answer. He thought of leaving men to watch over the bodies. He discarded the notion as ridiculous, and far too risky. It was doubtful they'd learn anything anyway.

"Let's get out of here, Shan. It is time to go home to our families, forget about the dead and rejoice in the living."

"Yes," Shan said, nodding. "We are gone long time."

- CHAPTER FIFTEEN -

SINCE THEY CACHED THE bodies, Tah had led them to higher and higher ground. The KNU had been decimated in the recent confrontation with the Burmese and were down to only seven men, two of them wounded. Earlier, Payne had tried to administer first aid, but they refused. The KNU seemed driven to put as much distance as possible between them and any Burmese Army patrols. McShane didn't blame them for that.

With Chan, the team's primary means of communicating with the KNU, now dead and the KNU at only half their original strength, McShane was uncertain how the team should proceed. Their options seemed limited to only two possible scenarios. Either they continued with their mission, and went on with the KNU to the camp to try to locate Slade, or abandoned the operation entirely.

After the firefights, he felt the operation was compromised. He doubted Rayburn, or anyone else, had expected they'd encounter so much resistance. While it wouldn't be a popular decision, he was opting for calling the operation off. He knew Rayburn and the Pentagon would be disappointed, because they were anxious to get to the bottom of the live sightings. But the last thing he wanted was to lose any of his team on what could be a wild goose chase anyway. He didn't think it would be too difficult to dissuade Rayburn. The mission wouldn't be a total loss. "B" Company in Lop

Buri could still airdrop the weapons and ammo and the team could stick around for a few days to offer any training the KNU might want.

McShane was deep in thought when Tah motioned everyone into a rocky formation of stone spires. The rocks completely enveloped them, towering above them as high as two and three story buildings. McShane noted that the monoliths provided excellent cover and concealment from any outside threat. He watched in awe as a KNU soldier, posted as a sentry by Tah, scampered up one of the spires as easily as a cat climbing a tree. It was obvious to McShane that the KNU were no strangers to the rocks.

The team un-shouldered their backpacks and settled against one of the boulders. McShane was famished. They'd been on the go since breakfast, taking only an occasional water break. He pulled out a foil packet of freeze-dried Chicken Alfredo he'd bought mail order from REI. He could barely stomach the Army's LRRP freeze-dried rations anymore and usually preferred to bring along his own civilian chow. The problem with any freeze-dried ration, however, was the same. They took water to reconstitute the food, and water was often scarce. This morning before they left, he had taken the time to pour hot tea water into the packet. The Chicken Alfredo was now the consistency of baby food.

If he was hungry, he could just imagine how Pike's stomach must be growling. He scooped out a mess of Alfredo with a plastic spoon he'd brought along and glanced over at Pike, who sat cross-legged, with his backpack opened. Reaching into his pack, he pulled out a couple of hardboiled eggs and a granola bar.

McShane chuckled. "Hungry, Charlie?"

"Nothing like a firefight to bring out the hunger in a man," Pike remarked, as he cracked one of the eggs on his knee.

"Any excuse is a good enough reason for you to eat, Charlie," said Lieutenant Hansen.

"Roger that, sir."

The KNU sat in a semi-circle a few meters out from the team. Tah tended to a wounded soldier's arm. The soldier squealed in pain when Tah tried to roll up the sleeve of his fatigue shirt.

"Shit," Colin Evans said. "I bet every Burmese within half a klick heard that. Hey, Travis, why don't you check out that guy's arm?"

"I tried earlier," Payne replied, "but they didn't want anything to do with White Man medicine."

"Well, try again, before the Burmese show up and add to your patient list."

"Yeah, okay, but give me a chance to finish this gourmet meal." Payne took a large bite out of the sandwich he'd made with some of the bread Chan had packed for them and sliced bananas the headman had given him. It reminded him of when he was a kid and his mother would make him peanut butter and banana sandwiches for lunch on the weekends. What he wouldn't give for some peanut butter to add to the otherwise bland sandwich. And a tall glass of cold milk. He wolfed down the rest of the sandwich in four huge bites then reached for his aid bag in his pack.

"Alright, Colin," Payne said, standing. "I'll try to bandage the guy's wounds. But there's nothing I can do if he doesn't want me to touch him. Besides, their jungle medicine is as good as ours sometimes."

"Yeah, well, shove a gag in his mouth if Tah does anymore work on him," Evans said. "I *would* like to get out of this God-forsaken jungle alive."

"Rather than bitch, why don't you give me a hand?" Payne asked.

"Okay," Evans said, standing slowly. "Hey, Charlie, Wade, get up off your lazy asses and give us a hand."

Pike groaned. "I'm not done eating."

"Tough. Get your sorry ass up. Wade, we may need to use your Thai expertise."

"No problem, Colin. I'd be honored to be your interpreter."

Lieutenant Hansen sat quietly eating a granola bar next to McShane. McShane watched the four men walk over to the KNU. Now was his opportunity to talk to his team commander about his thoughts on continuing the mission. Now that he'd eaten, however, and they were secure in the rocky fortress, his stance on calling the show off had softened somewhat. Nevertheless, he needed some feedback.

"L.T., I've been thinking," McShane began. "I'd like to talk something over with you."

Hansen stuffed the last of the bar in his mouth and turned toward his team sergeant. Ever since the firefight, he'd been doing some thinking of his own. It was the first time he'd come under fire and he was still a little unnerved. As a member of a Special Forces "A" team, he understood he could be called on at a moment's notice to engage a hostile force. But what he hadn't been prepared for mentally was facing a force that during their mission planning hadn't been considered a hostile threat. And he certainly didn't believe the mission was worth losing a single team member.

"Go ahead, Steve." In the field, military courtesy was on hold.

"Earlier," McShane began, "I was thinking we should radio "B" company and tell them our mission was compromised, we were being tracked by Burmese army patrols, and were unable to complete our mission without putting the team in unnecessary danger. I still think that, but I'm also wondering if that isn't the chicken shit way out. I'm short, less than a couple months left in the army. But I don't want that to cloud my judgment. On the other hand, I'd sure be pissed if I got anybody's ass shot off in Burma, looking for someone that likely doesn't exist, or is so well hidden we'd never find him anyway. Do you understand my dilemma?"

Hansen grinned and nodded his head. "I do, because I was pretty much thinking the same thing. We may not be so lucky the next time around. Half the KNU we started out with are now out of the picture, so we don't have as much firepower as before. If we do find ourselves backed up against a wall, any sort of Bright Light rescue operation would be at least an hour away. Yes, I see where you're coming from, but I'm not so certain we should give up just yet. I have a feeling we're very close to finding out the truth."

McShane stretched, arching his back, and locked his hands behind his head. "Damn, my back is sore. I'm more out of shape than I thought." He released his hands and straightened his back. "You may be right, L.T. We're so close that it would be a shame to turn back. We'll keep on, and do our damnedest to avoid contact with the Burmese. If we can do that, we should be in good shape. But if contact is unavoidable, we'll have to reassess the situation."

"I'll go along with that plan. We can't be too far away from the village now."

"Yeah, but these unexpected delays have really slowed us down. I don't know if we'll make it by dark and with the AO crawling with Burmese, I don't want to do any traveling at night. It's not something I'm overly excited about, but we may have to RON somewhere in the jungle."

Hansen stood then bent over and touched his toes. He was beginning to feel the effects of the long march, too. It had been a while since the team humped a ruck over such rugged terrain. He held the position for a few seconds and then straightened.

"We should get movin' then."

"Let's see how Payne is doing with the wounded," McShane suggested.

The two wounded soldiers sat against a boulder with their fatigue shirts off. As McShane and Hansen approached, McShane noticed that the shoulder wound in one of the KNU had already been bandaged. Payne worked on the other soldier, cleaning a gash in his bicep with a cotton swab. The team stood in a semi-circle around their medic, observing closely. As he worked, Payne described what he was doing. Great real-world training, McShane thought.

"How much longer?" McShane asked.

"I'm about done for now," he replied, unrolling a length of gauze. "Got 'em cleaned up pretty well, I think. Their wounds weren't all that bad." Payne began wrapping gauze around the young KNU's arm. "Luckily, the gunshots were through-and-through, so I won't have to perform surgery. I'll check their wounds tomorrow to make sure there isn't any infection before I sew 'em up. Give me a minute or two to get this guy bandaged and I'll be set to go." He turned toward the team, who now seemed antsy. "All right, class dismissed."

"We're lucky to have Travis as our medic," Pike said to Everett and Evans as they returned to grab their equipment. "Did you see how quickly he got those guys patched up?"

"Yep, he's damn good," Everett added. "Saw him one time in Salvador, back in '83, save this young Salvadorean soldier from bleeding to death when the kid, barely seventeen, blew off his own leg when he dropped a live grenade and was too scared to run. The blast tore off the right leg right up to the hip. The kid was screaming for his mother so loud that I had to gag him. I had to shoot him up with three syrettes of morphine to calm him down enough so Doc could work on him. Took every clamp he had in his bag to stop the bleeding. The kid's goddamn blood was everywhere. But Ol' Doc Payne got the kid stable enough to evac him to a field hospital. A month later, he was hobbling around on crutches. I can sometimes still hear him hollering, 'Madre! Madre!'"

"Wow," Pike said, shaking his head. "Hope that never happens to me."

Evans chuckled. "You're too stupid to get yourself blown up."

"Now what's that supposed to mean, Colin?" Pike asked. "*You're* the weapons man, not me. And we all know what dumb asses they are." Pike gave Evans a playful shove.

"Alright, listen up," McShane said to the team as they approached. "With all the delays, I don't know if we're going to make it to the village by nightfall."

The team sighed audibly. "Yes, I know, I wanted to get there too, but with all the Burmese in the area, we don't want to get into too much of a hurry. We can't be too careful. So, as of right now, there's a chance we may have to RON somewhere. Any questions?"

Pike turned toward Everett, and Everett glanced over at Evans. They shrugged.

"I guess not," Pike answered, "but I think I can speak for the others when I say, let's get the fuck out of here."

"Get your gear and we will. Everett, tell Tah we're moving out and that I want half his men in front of us and the rest following us."

"Done," Everett said, and turned on his heels to find Tah.

"Pike, give Doc a hand packing up his aid bag," McShane ordered.

Without a word, Pike hoisted his backpack onto his shoulders. But before Pike had a chance to help Payne, he'd already packed and was standing by the others, ready to move out. He was soon followed by Tah and the KNU. The team fell in behind the KNU as they headed toward the entrance to the stone fortress.

Re-entering the thick jungle, McShane couldn't help reflecting on the importance, or unimportance, of their mission. One minute he was enthusiastic, and the next he wanted to call the whole thing off. Earlier he'd told Hansen they were too close to their objective to quit, but now he wasn't so sure. He just couldn't shake the feeling of dread that their troubles were far from over. Long ago he'd learned not to discount his instincts. It was imperative they proceed with extreme caution to avoid any further confrontation. It was his responsibility to get his team out of Burma safely and he would do whatever it took.

- C H A P T E R S I X T E E N -

SLADE AND THE KNU began their descent into a narrow mountain valley surrounded by craggy ridges and thick jungle forests. Slade knew the valley was so remote and hard to find that their village was safe from roving Burmese patrols. Over two hundred KNU lived in small camps and villages in and around the valley. Even if an enemy patrol did venture too close, the KNU had dozens of sentries posted at every possible approach to the village, hiding in the jungle and behind rocks. They passed the first KNU checkpoint, some half-dozen kilometers from the valley. His spirits soared, knowing he would soon be reunited with his wife and daughter.

The men waved as the guards stepped into the open from their hideaways. The sentries seemed particularly pleased to see them, as they smiled broadly and waved back. No doubt, Slade thought, they had learned of the firefights with the Burmese soldiers. Despite their remoteness, the village learned of news rapidly from other KNU villages. Villages would pass along useful information to the KNU guards who would, in turn, radio their reports to their village. It was a primitive way to communicate, but highly effective. In the ten years he'd been here, Burmese patrols had never made it closer than four miles without meeting heavy resistance and being forcibly turned away.

Slade couldn't wait to see Soon and his daughter Mar. Time had seemed to pass slowly lately. He felt as though he'd been gone for months instead of a few weeks. He'd grown so weary of the fighting. For more than two decades, he had been in someone else's fight. It was time to find peace. He'd earned it.

He would again talk to Soon about moving across the border into a refugee camp. In a camp, they would have access to medical help from volunteer medical missionary groups. In Thailand, Mar would have a better chance for a decent life.

It had been so long since his disappearance in Laos. He felt there was no chance anyone could possibly believe he was alive and certainly would not be able to recognize him. He knew he'd been forgotten by everyone, except perhaps his Aunt Virginia and his brother Paul, if they were still alive. Eventually, he, Soon, and Mar could move into Chiang Rai, a large town south of the Burmese border. He could easily find a job teaching English, or even guiding foreign tourists on hill tribe treks into the mountains.

As they entered the village, he caught sight of Soon in a crowd of villagers who had assembled to greet them. She held Mar's hand. When his daughter saw him, she broke away from her mother. Mar pushed her way through the villagers and leaped into her father's outstretched arms. He was so exhausted that she nearly knocked him over. He squeezed her tight and kissed her cheek.

"Father, I missed you so much. What took you so long?"

"I missed you too, sweetheart." He ignored the question and lowered her to the ground. Soon ran up to him and they embraced.

Slade couldn't believe how good it felt to hold her after such a long absence. He ran his hands through her waist-length, black hair, in long, even strokes. As with most Karen, she was short, barely five feet tall. She wore a loose-fitting green blouse with a long hand-woven black and red skirt. He rested his chin on top of her head and thought briefly about unwrapping the skirt where they stood. But he'd waited this long; he could wait awhile longer, after Mar was asleep in their two-room hut.

A sudden tug at his fatigue pants disturbed his thoughts. He released his hold on Soon and glanced down. Mar looked up at him with brown almond eyes.

"What, Mar?"

"I want to show you what mother made me for my birthday."

"Oh, shit," he muttered to himself in English. He rarely spoke English anymore, except maybe when he was alone and talked to himself. He had been away for her birthday. He felt guilty for not remembering.

Slade grabbed Mar just beneath her spindly arms and lifted her above his head. She laughed hysterically as he spun her around in his large hands. "Happy birthday, little one. I am sorry I wasn't here to celebrate with you, but Daddy had to chase the bad Burmese soldiers away."

"I know, Daddy, now put me down," she hollered, kicking her feet frantically. "Put me down!" Slade held her aloft a moment longer then lowered her to the ground. When her feet hit the dirt, she darted off to their hut, scampered up the bamboo ladder, and disappeared inside. A short time later, she returned holding a hand-woven black and red coat. She held it up.

"Mother made it for the cold winter nights," she said proudly.

Slade turned the jacket over in his hands, studying the intricate designs stitched into the fabric. Soon sewed beautifully, he knew, but she'd outdone herself this time.

"It is beautiful, Mar. Your mother is the best seamstress in all of Burma." He glanced over at his wife. She blushed over his compliment. "Maybe she will make me one for the long winter nights, too."

"I will, if you promise not to be gone so much."

He turned and smiled. She was so beautiful. All he wanted was for them to be safe and live a quiet, simple life. As soon as they were alone, he would talk to her about moving as soon as possible. It was really their only option if they wanted a life without fear of harassment from the Burmese military and a future for Mar. He kissed her tenderly on the lips.

"That is all I want, too."

They walked together toward their hut at the far end of the village, with Mar between them, holding their hands. His KNU patrol made their way with their families to their homes. The villagers who'd lost sons in the firefights walked away sadly, solemnly. They would mourn their losses later, but tonight, Slade knew, the entire village would gather for a welcome home celebration.

The village would feast on a roast pig wrapped in banana leaves that had been cooking since the villagers got word they were returning. After the feast, the villagers would dance around a roaring bonfire to the haunting sounds made by an elder blowing into a long, bamboo tube.

Their hut was constructed no differently than others in the village. It stood a couple of meters off the ground on teak poles. This kept water out of the hut during the heavy monsoon rains that flooded the village during the summer months. The floor was made of thick bamboo poles lashed together with hemp, while the walls were made of woven bamboo strips. A roof of broad, green banana leaves kept them dry.

Slade lifted Mar above his head and set her down on the bamboo deck. He allowed Soon to walk up the bamboo ladder first then followed closely behind. He followed her swaying shape, encased to the ankles by her tight tribal dress. His body ached for hers. They would have to convince Mar to take a nap before the celebration tonight.

Entering the hut through its low opening, Slade was suddenly overwhelmed by fatigue. It had been days since he got any real sleep. It was all he could do to keep from collapsing on their sleeping mat, in the corner of the room. Soon stirred the contents of a large pot over the hut's fire pit. She had cooked something special for him. If he fell asleep she would understand, but he loved her too much to disappoint her by going to sleep. Mar sat cross-legged in front of the fire, watching her mother. He sat down next to her and she snuggled against him.

"Father, why do you have to go off and fight all the time?" She asked in her soft voice.

"I don't go all the time."

"It seems like you do. I haven't seen you since the last full moon."

He took her tiny, delicate hand in his. It looked so small in his large, calloused palm. He closed his fingers around her hand and squeezed lightly. "Well, I don't mean to be gone so much. I would like to change that so we can be together more."

Soon glanced up from the pot and studied her husband carefully. She wondered what he was thinking, how could their life possibly change as long as the Burmese persecuted the Karen people? She hoped he wasn't considering moving to a relocation camp in Thailand again. While the camps were safer, without the constant dangers of being attacked, she also knew from friends who'd relocated, then returned, that the camps were cramped and crowded. Food from the Thai government was meager, and there was little chance they would ever have land of their own. But she also knew he had long ago grown weary of the fighting, and that he was concerned for their safety. They would have to talk later, after Mar had gone to sleep.

Slade turned toward his wife. "Soon, whatever is in that pot smells wonderful. I am starved for real food."

"Me, too." Mar added.

"I am pleased you are both so hungry. It is a stew made from a chicken I killed this morning. Hand me your bowls."

Slade handed his bowl to Soon. "Wonderful." He smacked his lips for his daughter. "Anything but dried fish. I don't think I want to eat that for a long, long time."

Mar crinkled her nose. "Dried fish, yuk. I hate it, too."

"Well, sometimes it is okay," Slade added. "It is very healthy for little girls. You need to grow up big and strong."

"I don't want to grow up big and strong," Mar said. "That's for the boys, so they can fight the Burmese."

"Yes, that is true, but you need to be strong so you can help your mother carry baskets of rice from the fields."

"I already do that, father."

He smiled fondly. "Yes, you do. Let's not worry about dried fish anymore." He reached for his steaming bowl, piled high with succulent pieces of stewed chicken, rice, and green vegetables and garlic he knew came from the village garden. "Your mother's chicken stew is much better than any yucky, dried fish."

Mar giggled and took her bowl from her mother's outstretched hand. They ate in silence. The only sounds were the grunting of their two sows beneath the hut, as they routed for overlooked scraps from the morning meal. Slade imagined he was making just as much noise as he gulped the stew in large mouthfuls. He hadn't realized he was so hungry.

I think this is your best stew ever, Soon."

"It is the same as always," she replied modestly as she refilled his bowl. "You are just hungry."

"Too much dried fish," Mar added, giggling louder than before.

"You are both right. I am hungry and yes, little one, too much fish. I thought we weren't going to talk about yucky fish anymore?"

Mar tilted her head downward in mock embarrassment. She lifted her eyes to meet his, and smiled coyly. "I am sorry, Daddy." Soon placed her hand over her mouth to disguise her laughter.

"Alright, you two, that is enough," Slade said, holding back his own laughter. He was giddy with happiness at finally being home, away from the dangers of patrolling in Burmese territory. He felt a tremendous urge to scoop them both into his arms and hug them. As he stood up, his attention was suddenly diverted to a sound unheard of in their village.

Moving hurriedly to the open doorway, he focused his gaze toward the mountains. He had hoped he'd been mistaken in what he heard. His heart sank when his fears were confirmed. As the sounds became more distinct, he clearly made out the unmistakable throb of a helicopter's rotor blades slicing through the humid air. Suddenly, the bloated outline of two Russian-manufactured Hind helicopters came into view. He hurriedly motioned Soon and Mar from behind the table.

"Quickly, go to the caves," he commanded calmly, as he grabbed his AK-47 and a bandolier of ammo.

Soon gave her husband a brief kiss on the cheek and took Mar's hand. They quickly descended the stairs and joined the other women, children and elderly as they headed for the labyrinth of caves in the limestone hillsides.

Slade wasn't concerned about their safety. They had practiced the drill many times. Food and water had been stockpiled in the caves for just such emergencies and there was no way a Burmese patrol or even a company-sized element could find their way into them. A twenty-man security element would accompany the villagers. From hidden emplacements carved into the cliffs, they could hold off hundreds of troops indefinitely.

Slade joined the men from his patrol and studied the approaching Hinds. They circled the rice fields in the valley. He swore to himself. This was the first time helicopters had intruded on their tiny village. The Burmese, he figured, must be tired of fighting them in the jungles, and more serious about eradicating them. Well, not without one hell of a fight, he thought. They had a few tricks of their own they were eager to show the Burmese.

Slade and his men headed for defensive positions in the rocks above. There were RPD light machine gun emplacements carved into the rocks. Each position had an escape route into a cave. In addition, they had a half-dozen RPG-7 rocket grenade launchers. The Burmese incursion might force them to relocate, or cause them to scatter and regroup into smaller villages, but Slade looked forward to making them first suffer a little humiliation.

They reached their positions just as the two helicopters swooped over the north end of the village. The door-gunners immediately opened fire, raking the bamboo huts with machine gun fire. Burmese soldiers leaned out open doorways and fired their AKs on full automatic. Pigs squealed as bullets tore their bodies apart.

The Hinds made two more passes, each time riddling the village with more gunfire. After the third pass, the helicopters set down in the village's vegetable garden and twenty Burmese soldiers from each helicopter poured out and dashed for the village, rifles blazing. Suddenly, Slade noticed another pair of Hinds approaching low over the mountains from the east. He couldn't worry about them just yet. He had a more immediate problem.

Slade couldn't believe the soldiers were acting so recklessly. They should have sensed something was wrong when they didn't encounter any resistance and been more cautious with their advance. Well, they'd soon regret their lack of professionalism.

From their vantage point, Slade and the KNU had perfect fields of fire, and would easily be able to cut the enemy to shreds. But first, he wanted to take care of the Hinds. Without them, the soldiers were doomed. It was something he'd learned in Vietnam. The NVA had targeted American helicopters on the ground, knowing that without them the U.S. soldiers were trapped.

Two KNU soldiers loaded their RPGs and took careful aim. Slade was confident they'd hit on the first attempt, but he also knew that the Hinds were slow; if they missed, they would have a second opportunity. The machine gun crews and all the other soldiers were poised to open fire. Slade had instructed the men to wait for the RPGs to fire before they opened up on the advancing Burmese.

Slade shook his head in amazement as the Burmese blindly rushed the village. None provided covering fire, and they were all bunched up. As the cluster of soldiers entered the village, Slade turned to the RPG grenadiers and nodded. Instantly, two rocket-propelled grenades spiraled toward the helicopters. The two KNU quickly reloaded.

The withering machine gun and automatic weapons fire that followed was an overwhelming roar of sound. Slade winced. It reminded him of a mad minute demonstration during basic training. He wished for ear protection.

One of the rockets hit the rotor shaft of the Hind on the paddy to their right. The blades broke loose from the shaft and spun through the air, felling several thin saplings. The other rocket fell shy of its mark, bursting in front of the open doorway. The blast did manage to kill the door gunner and wounded two soldiers standing nearby.

As the Hind started to lift off, the KNU soldiers fired again. The helicopter only managed a couple of meters before one rocket detonated between the two pilots, blowing out the front half of the helicopter. The other rocket burst inside the cabin, killing the remaining door gunner and crew chief. Slade grinned. But now they had to contend with the other rapidly approaching helicopters.

Slade signaled the KNU to stop firing. The cordite stench was so heavy he had to suppress a sneeze. He scanned the village over the rock precipice.

The ground was littered with dead and dying Burmese army soldiers. Not one was standing. He almost felt sorry for them. He knew the majority were just young boys conscripted away from their families by a tyrannical government to fight an enemy they didn't even know.

Well, better them than us, he decided.

It was time to focus on the other two helicopters. They hovered several meters north of the burning hulks of the first two Hinds. The KNU soldiers raised their RPGs to their shoulders once again and in unison depressed the triggers. This time, their aim was dead on and the choppers erupted into brilliant fireballs, explosions flinging burning Burmese soldiers into the air.

-CHAPTER SEVENTEEN-

THEY HAD TRAVELED FOR more than an hour along a narrow path weaving in and out of the jungle, surrounded by jagged, volcanic rock formations. McShane was tired and hoped they'd stop soon. He pulled his canteen from his rucksack and took a long swallow of tepid, iodine-flavored water. Thank God he was getting short and would never have to experience that taste again.

As he replaced the canteen, his attention was drawn to the skyline. The entire team, as well as the KNU, gazed upwards at nearly the same instant. The KNU slowed then stopped. They heard clearly, off to the west, the sounds of at least two helicopters approaching the valley. Suddenly, the KNU were on the move again, now double-timing along the narrow path.

Moments later, they heard two explosions, followed immediately by an intense barrage of automatic weapons fire. McShane was thankful he wasn't on the receiving end. Realizing their village was under attack, the KNU further picked up the pace. Now, almost at a dead run, they heard two more explosions, much louder this time. McShane prayed they weren't too late to help.

He contemplated radioing the "B" team who, along with Thai Special Forces, had formed a Bright Light team. They were on standby near the border, after he'd radioed the night before. However, he quickly dismissed that idea; they were in capable hands with the KNU.

The KNU abruptly left the trail, turning in to a thicket of dense scrub brush. Spiny thorns tore at their arms. Once they passed through the brush, they came to a small, rocky clearing. He caught a glimpse of two KNU sentries crouched behind some rocks ten meters or so above them. They waved. Entering a narrow opening in the rocks, McShane suddenly found himself in a cave. Up ahead, someone carried a kerosene lamp.

The cave reeked of bat guano, but was cool and damp, a welcome relief from the heat and humidity. The narrow, claustrophobic limestone passageway pressed in tightly, scraping his shoulders and already scratched forearms. In many places, he was forced to stoop to avoid cracking his skull on the jagged cave ceiling. Overwhelmed by the stench from the bat shit, he fought off waves of nausea. He now longed to be outside, despite the heat.

Thirty meters ahead, he made out a sliver of daylight, filtering through a narrow opening. The soldiers in the lead began snaking their way through the hole. As McShane waited his turn, he was relieved he hadn't vomited all over the soldier in front of him.

Harsh sunlight momentarily blinded him as he stooped low to navigate the tiny cave exit. Once outside, he stood on a narrow ledge a couple hundred meters above the ground. He couldn't see the village, but could clearly hear bursts of small arms fire.

The KNU were already making their way along the ledge and onto a trail that ascended the steep cliff. He waited for the remainder of the team to exit, noting that the gunfire was less intense than before. Only a few scattered shots were audible by the time Charlie Pike poked his head out into the daylight.

"Fuck this shit," Pike muttered, yanking at his rucksack, which had snagged on a rock.

Travis Payne was right behind him. "Get your lard ass movin'. I'm going to puke if I spend another second in this stinkin' cave." He gave Pike a light shove.

"Gimme a break, Travis! My fuckin' ruck's stuck on somethin'." He wriggled his shoulders, finally freeing the ruck.

Learning from Pike's mistake, the remainder of the team took off their rucks and handed them through to McShane and Pike. Without the bulk of their rucksacks, Payne, Evans, Everett, and Lieutenant Hansen exited easily.

Re-shouldering their packs, the team watched in awe as the five rear-security KNU soldiers scampered quickly through the opening without so much as touching the cave walls.

"Being small does have its advantages," Pike said to no one in particular as he drank from his canteen.

"We're laggin'. Let's catch up with the others," McShane ordered.

The KNU had already scurried down the track with the grace of alpine sheep. Unfamiliar with the steep terrain, the team had a rougher time, oftentimes slipping on loose rocks. After nearly ten minutes, the track leveled off and the team was able to move easily and at a swifter pace. There was no sign of the KNU soldiers who'd gone ahead of them. By now, McShane figured, they'd already reached the village.

Two soldiers from the rear security element came forward to lead the way. McShane was relieved they'd taken over. He was growing anxious, unsure of what to expect when they arrived at the village. He wondered if the Burmese forces had slaughtered all the villagers, including Slade.

The rocky terrain suddenly changed. They entered a dark, dense forest of banana and mango trees. They heard short bursts of automatic weapons fire ahead. Their journey was almost over. The KNU soldier ahead of him turned and pointed to his AK's selector switch. McShane understood instantly and shifted the switch on his CAR-15 to auto. He passed on the signal to the others.

A few minutes later, they entered the outskirts of the village. It was deathly quiet. There were bodies of dead Burmese scattered throughout the village. McShane spotted dozens of KNU soldiers pursuing several Burmese soldiers across a rice paddy toward the jungle a couple hundred meters away. Three KNU paused, raised their rifles, and fired at two Burmese, who collapsed face first into the paddy.

It was difficult for McShane to be sure, because of the distance, but one of the KNU appeared much larger than the others. At least a good head taller, he estimated. In addition, the soldier had longish grey hair. He strained to get a better look, and was about to grab the binoculars from his ruck when the soldier disappeared into the jungle. McShane wondered if the gray-haired soldier could possibly be Slade.

McShane shrugged off what he'd just witnessed and turned his attention back to the village. As he scanned the bodies, he realized there weren't any villagers among the dead. Not a single man, woman, or child. He wondered what had become of them. Their KNU escort was moving among the fallen Burmese soldiers, collecting their weapons and ammo belts. The team worked their way cautiously among the bloodied corpses, keeping alert for any living soldiers who may have escaped the blood bath.

McShane noticed Payne kneeling beside the body of a Burmese soldier who looked to be fifteen or sixteen. As he approached, his medic looked up at him sadly.

"Why is it always the young sent off to die?" Payne asked, turning his attention back to the soldier, whose right arm had been torn away from his shoulder by machine gun fire. "I'll bet you a month's pay this kid never got laid."

"I don't know, Travis," McShane replied, shaking his head. "It seems like it's always been that way. Vietnam was like that. Average age there was something like eighteen or nineteen."

"Maybe that's why I became a medic," Payne said, standing next to McShane.

"And why's that?"

"To try to save kids like this one."

"That's very noble, but right now we need to think about ourselves," McShane said. "Get Everett, go over to Tah, and have him ask what the hell is going on and where is everybody."

Lieutenant Hansen, along with Evans and Pike, crossed through the village; they walked toward the smoldering wreckage of the helicopters, following four KNU soldiers. They braced their CARs against their shoulders, poised for action.

As Everett approached, Tah gestured toward the jungle on the opposite side of the rice paddies, speaking rapid fire Thai. They spoke for a time then Everett returned to McShane's side.

"What'd he say, Wade?"

"His Thai isn't the best, but he thinks it is. I had to tell him to slow down and speak slower. The bottom line is the KNU in the village blew up the four helicopters that brought the troops in. They killed all the Burmese except the ones in the last chopper. Those, he said, fled into the jungle and are now being hunted down. They don't want anyone getting out alive to tell what happened here today. Later, they'll disassemble the choppers and hide the pieces in the jungle."

"Does he know anything about the white guy who lives here?"

Everett turned back to Tah and there was a brief verbal exchange. "He says he doesn't know."

"Damn." McShane had pondered whether the team should follow the KNU into the jungle and seek out the grey-haired guy. That might have settled a lot of questions about who the man was and if, in fact, he was Slade. But he'd decided against jeopardizing the team. There were still sporadic bursts of gunfire from the jungle, and he again had to remind himself that it wasn't their fight.

"What did he say happened to the villagers?" McShane asked.

"They're hiding in caves until it's safe to return," Everett replied.

"Radio the 'B' team that we have reached our objective. Tell them about the fight with the Burmese, and that we'll wait until the KNU return to the village." McShane paused, wondering what additional information Everett should pass on. "Have them stand by. They may have to come in hot, just in case more Burmese return and we get in a bind."

"I'm probably going to have to move up the mountain to get any reception, but I'll try down here first," Everett replied.

"Take Pike and a couple of KNU from the security element."

Everett nodded, walked over to a hut and began assembling the satellite antenna on the raised porch. He gazed upwards, searching for an unobstructed view of the southern skies. There was a small opening in the jungle canopy about thirty degrees overhead, but he was doubtful it was the correct azimuth. In order to communicate with the "B" team, he needed to position the antenna in perfect alignment with an orbiting military satellite.

He decided not to go through the trouble of completing his setup. When they were descending the mountain, he recalled noticing a rock slab near the military crest of the mountain that likely would be a perfect location. He hurriedly repacked the dish and headed toward the still smoldering choppers to get Pike.

As Everett approached, Lieutenant Hansen photographed one of the downed helicopters, while Pike and Payne rummaged through the contents of another, searching for documents that might prove useful to the Thai military. They'd already completed the search of one of the Hinds. The cockpit was so badly burned, including the pilots still strapped in their seats, that they found nothing of value. The chopper they were now investigating had suffered less damage.

"Find anything, Charlie?" Everett asked.

Pike had unfastened the Burmese co-pilot's shoulder harness, allowing his charred body to topple to the ground, and was reaching under the seat. He withdrew a leather briefcase and held it up.

"Letters from home," Pike said, grinning.

"Give 'em to Travis. I need you to help me set up the radio."

Pike nodded, handed the satchel to Payne, and then joined Everett for the trek up the mountainside. Tah assigned three KNU to accompany them. One of the KNU led the way, while the other two followed.

-CHAPTER EIGHTEEN-

SLADE BRUSHED A TANGLE of vines away from his field of vision and peered into the jungle foliage. Three Burmese soldiers clawed frantically at the undergrowth, trying to flee their pursuers. Slade wanted to pity them, but if they escaped to tell their commanders what had happened at the village, more Burmese soldiers would come. The next time, they might not be as fortunate as they had been today.

Without hesitation or remorse, for he knew that if the tables were turned the Burmese wouldn't think twice of ending his or any of the KNU's lives, he raised his AK and squeezed off four short bursts. The soldiers crumpled to the ground without a cry. Slade lowered his weapon, changed magazines then pushed through the thicket to hunt down more of the enemy. He gave the fallen soldiers a cursory glance, checking for signs of life. From the severity of their head wounds, he knew they wouldn't trouble anyone ever again.

Several shots muffled by dense undergrowth came from his right front. He headed toward the gunfire to investigate. He hoped the Burmese hadn't gotten the jump on his KNU. As he neared where he thought the shots had been fired from, another volley suddenly erupted just meters away.

Rounds cracked terrifyingly overhead, chipping away at limbs and leaves. It was impossible to determine who was firing. He fell behind a stump, fixing the sights of his AK on a point where he thought the gunfire had originated. As abruptly as it had begun, it ceased. The jungle was eerily silent. There were no sounds of movement, or moans from any wounded. Baffled, he began to inch forward from his position, low-crawling toward a large banyan tree that would afford more cover and concealment.

Once safely behind the tree, he slowly stood, keeping an eye out for enemy soldiers or friendly KNU. The foliage was so thick he could make out nothing beyond a few meters. There could be a hundred Burmese soldiers hidden in the jungle and he wouldn't know it. That notion was frightening.

He glanced over his shoulder in the direction from which he had just come. There was nothing, just a mass of dull green. The silence began to nag at him, and suddenly he was concerned. He wondered if everyone had been killed and he was the only one left. That was a sobering thought. All he wanted now was to be free of his claustrophobic surroundings and hold Soon and Mar tightly to him.

Gradually, he began to step backwards. He didn't dare risk penetrating deeper into the jungle where visibility was nonexistent. The villagers never ventured this far into the jungle. They thought it too dense, and they feared evil spirits in its dank depths. He had always dismissed their beliefs as superstition, but now he tended to agree with them. If evil lurked anywhere, it was there.

When he reached the tree where he'd first hidden, he turned and started to make his way out of the jungle. He'd head back toward the village and hopefully link up with other KNU. The foliage was now much thinner, burned off years before to clear the land for farming, and travel was less difficult.

He could just make out the tilled cornfields and some of the larger huts through the thinning vegetation. The smoldering hulks of the downed Hinds also came into view. The downing of the helicopters had been a great victory for the KNU. However, he didn't want it to go to their heads, make them feel invincible.

He thought he spotted several men milling around the helicopters, and figured it was some of his KNU. But then, suddenly, they turned and walked away in a single file in the direction of the mountains behind the village. A number of them appeared much taller than others. He thought that was just his eyes faulty focus on distant objects. His eyes had been failing the last few years. He'd find out soon enough, after he was reunited with Soon and Mar.

A sudden noise caused him to freeze in his tracks. It sounded like someone tripping, somewhere off to his left. He swung his gaze in the direction of the sound. He stared hard. At first he couldn't make out anything, but as his eyes grew accustomed to the unfamiliar surroundings, he began to make out a particular shape. His heart nearly stopped when he realized what he was looking at.

Three Burmese soldiers crouched behind the remnants of a fallen tree he'd cut up years before when the land was cleared. The wood was nearly engulfed in vines. With their green fatigues, they were nearly undetectable, blending as one with the vine-covered log. They were fully aware of him, slowly raising their weapons.

"Not now, not today," he muttered to himself. Thoughts of his wife and daughter spun through his mind. The realization that he might die was overwhelming. But not without a fight, he thought. He began to take aim, but saw the Burmese already had him in their sights. He started to squeeze off a burst, but felt two searing, nearly simultaneous pains pass through his shoulder and chest. He toppled over backwards.

* * *

Everett and Pike returned with their KNU escort thirty minutes later. McShane and the others still rummaged through the Hinds. Everett walked up to his team leader, who sat on the edge, leafing through a magazine.

"I didn't know you could get *Time* magazine out here," Pike said, grinning.

"Actually, it's not *Time*; it's *Playboy*," McShane replied.

"Bullshit."

"Well, close. The Burmese edition." McShane held the front cover of the magazine up to his face, displaying a grainy, out-of-focus picture of two topless Burmese girls in their teens.

"I wonder if their articles are as informative as *Playboy's*," Pike said.

McShane grinned slyly. "Oh, you're one of *those* guys who reads *Playboy* for its articles, huh?"

"Of course."

McShane turned to Everett. "Wade, what did you get from the "B" team?

"They want us to avoid any further contact with the Burmese and pull back to the nearest possible LZ for an immediate extraction. They don't like the idea of us tangling with the Burmese military and creating an international incident."

"I don't blame them," McShane said. "I think we've taken our job about as far as it's gonna go. If Slade is alive, living out here in the jungle, then that must be what he wants. If he'd wanted to come home, he'd have done it long ago. Either that, or he's dead."

Suddenly, McShane was interrupted by the rapid pop-pop sounds of automatic weapons fire from deep inside the jungle across the field.

"Shit," McShane muttered as he tossed the magazine into the cockpit of the Hind.

Everett and Pike dropped to one knee and took cover behind the chopper fuselage. They trained their CAR's toward the jungle. Hansen and Payne fell to their bellies and crawled underneath the Hind.

McShane peered from behind the nose of the helicopter, scanning the jungle for signs of enemy movement. He guessed the KNU from the village had found more Burmese soldiers. Well, the KNU had proved they could take care of themselves. They didn't need the team's help.

Realizing there wasn't any real threat to the team, Hansen and Payne moved out from the helicopter and crouched next to McShane.

"What do you think, Steve?" Lieutenant Hansen asked, brow furrowed.

"Let's get the fuck out of here. We'll get our KNU escort and head for the nearest LZ. With any luck at all, we can be back at camp for a cold Singha before the sun sets."

-CHAPTER NINETEEN-

FROM THEIR VANTAGE POINT near the entrance to a small limestone cave high in the cliffs surrounding the village, Soon and Mar saw the men who looked like her husband leave their village and move swiftly up the trail that would take them back into Thailand. Soon didn't understand why they didn't wear uniforms, but carried rifles. She wondered if they had come to the village in search of her husband.

After a long pause in the fighting, the villagers emerged from hiding. They were pleased to see KNU soldiers coming from the jungle and not Burmese. They guessed their men must have been victorious over the enemy soldiers. They made their way down into the village, keeping a wary eye on the jungle.

As she held Mar's hand, steadying her descent over the craggy terrain, Soon thought hard about what had happened today. What would have happened if the KNU hadn't been there to shoot down the enemy helicopters? They easily could all have been killed or driven away into the jungle.

Many times her husband had talked to her about moving to Thailand. But she loved her village, and always talked him out of it; she feared living as a refugee. But after today, she had to think about Mar and her future, and less about her own desires. With the Burmese increasing their attacks on the KNU and their village, she understood they could no longer live in the peace they had enjoyed for so many years. She knew what had to be done. As soon as she saw her husband, she would tell him her plan.

There was something else she had decided in the cave. She wanted to learn more about her husband. He never talked about himself, even when she asked him about his family and his life before they met. He had always avoided answering her. After a time, she didn't bother him with such questions. Still, she wanted to know about his family. Was his father as kind to him as he was to Mar? Did he have any brothers or sisters? What was the village like where he grew up? Did they have to fight enemy soldiers? There were so many things she wanted to know. Once she told him her decision to go to Thailand, she would try to get him to talk.

As Soon and Mar entered the outskirts of the village, they noticed clusters of KNU soldiers, some bloodied from wounds, returning to the village. Most were smiling, some even laughing, as they relived among themselves their victories over the Burmese aggressors. This she took as a good sign. Hopefully, the enemy had been driven out for good. But she knew in her heart the Burmese would be back, stronger than ever. Mar suddenly broke from her hold and ran through the village in search of her father.

Soon grew worried when she didn't see her husband. Maybe he was helping with the wounded. She walked over to one of the Hinds and gazed out across the field toward the jungle. Soldiers were still making their way out, but she didn't see any sign of her husband. She walked up to two soldiers she knew from the village.

"Have you seen my husband?"

One of the men frowned. "Yes, they are bringing him out now."

Soon didn't understand what she was hearing. "What do you mean, bringing him out?"

"We're sorry, but he was badly wounded."

Soon raised her hand to her mouth and gasped. "Where did you see him?" she asked, her voice cracking.

"They were taking him to the headman's hut. The white nurse and village shaman are helping him."

They were referring to the woman her husband had told her was from Doctors Without Borders. She was a nurse, he had explained, something like a shaman, and came from a country called France. The woman was very beautiful, with long, straw-colored hair, the same color as her husband's, when they first met. She visited once a month for two days, treating the villagers who were too sick to be helped by the shaman. The woman had once given Mar some medicine that made her feel better after only one day. She trusted the nurse would not let her husband die. She hurried toward the headman's hut in the center of the village.

The hut's only illumination was from a kerosene lantern hanging by a wire from a bamboo rafter. It took Soon's eyes a moment to adjust to the dim light. Eventually, she made out her husband's lean figure, lying on a bamboo mat on the floor directly below the lantern. The white nurse knelt over his chest, cutting away his shirt with scissors, while the village shaman uttered a prayer to the Elephant God, the most powerful of all the Gods of the forest.

She quietly moved to the mat and knelt opposite the nurse. The nurse smiled at Soon, which gave her some comfort. Perhaps his injuries were not all that bad. There was a little blood on her husband's chest when the nurse pulled away his shirt. Her husband groaned, and then grew silent as if asleep. She laid her hand on his forehead and his eyes fluttered open. When he saw she was by his side, he smiled.

"I'm sorry, Soon," Slade said, then closed his eyes again.

"Do not be sorry, my husband. You will be well soon and we can go to Thailand with Mar. I love you." He smiled again without opening his eyes.

"Please get me the water on the fire so I can wash his wounds," the nurse said to Soon in near perfect Karen. There was a black, cast-iron pot on the coals of a cook fire in the center of the hut. Soon brought over the pot and placed it beside the nurse.

"Your husband was very lucky. The enemy bullets only hit the fleshy part of his body, not the important parts that a man needs to live. I will clean the wounds with medicine that will kill all the poison. He will probably be able to be out of bed in two or three days."

Soon smiled and took the warm, damp cloth from the nurse. She began wiping away the blood.

* * *

When the team reached the crest of the cliffs overlooking the valley and the village, McShane paused and took it all in. What a beautiful place, he thought, so lush, green and peaceful. Before the Burmese discovered it, the village must have been a wonderful place to live. Now, it was a scene of death and destruction.

The villagers, he knew, would likely have to move because the Burmese would no doubt return with a larger and stronger force. Hopefully, for the sake of their survival, the villagers would relocate to a refugee camp in Thailand, or start a village far from the valley. But he suspected many of the KNU soldiers would remain behind and continue to fight.

McShane felt as though they were deserting the villagers, and that the team should help in some way. Perhaps in a perfect world, they would. The Karen people had been taking care of themselves for centuries. He trusted they'd find a solution to their troubles without the team's interference. At least that was what he wanted to believe.

The team traveled south along some of the same trails and animal tracks they'd used to get to the village. Every hour or so they stopped for a five minute break. When there was only half an hour of daylight remaining, Lieutenant Hansen and McShane agreed they should RON, now that they had crossed over the mountain peak separating Thailand from Burma. They also agreed it was too late for a helicopter extraction. They'd have ample time to find an LZ in the morning.

After Everett called in their position to the "B" team, outlining their plan to find an LZ the following day, the team gathered inside a cluster of large rocks and dwarf banyan trees growing from fissures in the stone. Once the sun had set, the mountain air grew cold. They were out of danger now, and Pike started a small fire. Silently, each team member set up their MSR backpacking stoves and began cooking their favorite freeze-dried meal. McShane had another Shrimp Alfredo from REI.

Pike, holding his hands palm down over the fire, was the first to break the silence. "I wish we could have found out who that dude was. It would have been nice to know if he was Slade, and maybe learned what happened to the rest of his team."

McShane poured the dry contents of the Alfredo packet into boiling water in his stainless steel MSR one-quart pot. He stirred the mixture for a moment with a plastic spoon.

"Actually, I think it's better this way," McShane said. "Can you imagine, after all these years, what a field day the press, the *New York Times*, the *L.A. Times*, the *San Francisco Chronicle*, would have after he was returned to the States? Slade would be a sideshow attraction like the bearded lady in a carnival or somethin'. He would have been asked more questions than there are grains of sand in the ocean. First there'd be a lengthy, probably weeks-long, military de-briefing. Then the papers would have gotten hold of him. What were you doing in Laos? Why were you captured? What happened to the others? Did you really desert to save yourself? How did you escape? What were you doing in Burma? Did you sell drugs? How much money did you make from the drugs? The questions would have been ruthless and relentless."

"Yeah, you're right, Steve," Pike conceded. "But it would have been cool to know. We could have just talked to him a little bit, then left. Nobody would have had to know. It could have been the team's little secret."

"I like it better the way it turned out," McShane said. "Not knowing, I think, is better."

* * *

Three days later, when Slade was able to move about on his own, Soon suggested they walk to the narrow creek that flowed lazily behind the north end of the village. Soon was pleased her husband had such a rapid recovery. He actually had wanted to get up the day after he was wounded, but she insisted he lie still for another couple of days. Now that he was on his feet, she felt the time was right to tell him her decision. The creek, she thought, would be perfect. It was quiet and peaceful.

She took his arms and guided him carefully over the rocky creek bottom to a large flat rock on the opposite side of the stream. Soon helped him to sit then took her place next to him. For a time, they just watched the clear water cascade over the boulders.

"I've made up my mind, Kevin," she finally said, squeezing his forearm lightly. "I do not think we should stay in the village any longer. It is not safe here anymore."

Slade couldn't have been more pleased. Though he loved his years in this tranquil valley, he had known for some time that Soon's village, her home since birth, was no place to raise their daughter. With the recent attacks by the Burmese Army, it was apparent the valley had become far too dangerous for them or any of the villagers to remain. When the Burmese choppers failed to return, he was certain an even larger Burmese force would be sent in to finish off the village and anyone in it once and for all.

"Yes, I know. For a long time I have felt the village was too dangerous. The Burmese want to rid their country of the KNU and all who support them. I fear the Burmese are preparing to mount another attack in the coming days. We must convince the elders it is no longer safe to stay, and leave for Thailand immediately."

Soon brushed a tear from her eye. "I should have listened to you before and left months ago. Then perhaps none of this would have happened."

"You cannot think of the past, my dear wife, but only of our future in Thailand, with Mar, where we can live happily, without constant fear of death."

He stood slowly and took her hand. "Come, we must speak with the village chief, and convince him that his people are in danger if they remain here. If he chooses to stay, then we will go on our own."

Slade spent the afternoon with Lao, the village chief, and several of the elders. They had fought the

Burmese for so many years that they didn't know what a peaceful existence was. It was difficult to convince them they should leave their home of fifty years or more. In the end, they agreed to leave it to individual villagers to decide who wanted to stay, and who wanted to go to Thailand.

The elders would likely stay, Slade knew. They were too old to make the arduous trek over the mountains and would rather die defending their village than live in a refugee camp, dependent on the Thai government. They wouldn't be as fortunate as Slade. He likely could get a job teaching English, and rent a place away from the refugee camp. Unfortunately, he also understood, he could never return to the United States. There would be far too many questions. The mountains of Thailand and Burma were now his home.

After his talk with the chief, Slade decided he, Soon, and Mar would leave in the morning. He feared the Burmese military was planning an immediate counter attack and he didn't want to press his luck by staying any longer than necessary. They would pack the few possessions they had, and carry them in rucksacks. Before they reached the border, he would cache his weapons in a safe place, for retrieval at a later date, if necessary. He prayed that day would never come.

That night, the villagers gathered around an enormous bonfire, feasting on roast pig and drinking rice wine. Some danced to the melodic sounds of the large bassoon-like bamboo instruments, while others quietly spoke among themselves, discussing the elder's decision.

Slade and Soon sat nearby on a bamboo bench, watching Mar dance with her friends. Earlier in the evening, he and Soon explained to her that they were moving to another village on the other side of the mountains.

"Will the others in the village be going with us?" she asked a little sadly, not fully comprehending the extent of the move and how it would affect the remainder of her life.

"We do not know who will go, or who will stay," her mother explained, "but it is now too dangerous here. The Burmese soldiers will come back one day soon and try to chase us away. Many more may die."

Mar nodded her head and then rejoined her friends by the fire. She had known no life other than this simple existence, Slade thought. He knew she would be terribly saddened to leave the village and especially her friends since birth. But this was for the best.

Later in the night, when the fire died, Lao, the village chief, approached Slade and Soon. He walked unsteadily, stumbling twice. Lao, Slade knew, loved rice wine and no doubt consumed his fair share. It wasn't the first time Slade had seen him in such a state.

Lao sat cross-legged in front of them, his head bowed. At first, Slade thought he'd fallen asleep, but then he raised his head and peered at Slade through narrowing eyes. When he finally spoke, Slade and Soon could barely make out what he was saying.

"The men will stay in the village," Lao began. "Women and children will go to Thailand. You will lead them. You have done enough for us, and our people are thankful. This is no longer your fight. You have trained our men well. One KNU is equal to ten Burmese soldiers. If they come back, we will kill them all. Tomorrow at first light, thirty of our best soldiers will go with you to the Thai border to make sure you are safe."

Without another word and before Slade could respond, Lao suddenly stood and stumbled toward his hut. Slade and Soon followed his progress to make certain he reached his hut safely, then turned to one another and smiled. The KNU escort eased Slade's mind, because it would be a difficult and dangerous journey over the mountains. But he knew his soldiers would be up to the task.

Slade took Soon's hand and together they walked slowly to their small hut for the last time. It saddened him that tonight would be their last time to sleep in the house he'd built with Soon's brother. But, at the same time, anticipating a new life without fear filled him with a joy he hadn't experienced since the day Mar was born.

The next morning, the villagers moving to Thailand stood in front of their huts, tearfully saying their goodbyes. The uncertainty of when the wives and children would be reunited with their husbands and adult sons made the farewells all the more difficult. Slade wished everyone would leave and abandon the village forever. Perhaps in a month or two, he prayed.

With the KNU soldiers split up evenly among the file of villagers, carrying their few meager belongings in large, elongated baskets strapped to their backs, they struck off up the trail that ascended the mountain slope. Slade walked up front with the lead element of KNU, men he'd known and fought with for more years than he cared to recall. Pru and Shan walked alongside him. Soon followed a short distance behind with Mar. Near the crest of the hill, Slade climbed atop a large rock formation and gazed one last time at the village.

THE END

ABOUT THE AUTHOR

Born in California, Kent White joined the Army during his second year of college. After Airborne and Special Forces weapons training, he was assigned to a top secret Studies and Observation Group, or SOG, unit in the Central Highlands of South Vietnam. Recipient of the Purple Heart and Bronze Star with "V" device, he writes from his experiences in SOG. He now lives on the West Coast of California.

GLOSSARY

AO: Area of Operations.

Arc Light: B-52 bombing mission.

BDA: Bomb Damage Assessment.

Bright Light: Code word for a POW, or other rescue operation.

CAR-15: A smaller version of the M-16 with a shortened barrel and telescoping, metal stock.

FOB: Forward Observation Base. There were four SOG FOBs located in Vietnam - Phu Bai, Da Nang, Kontum and Ban Me Thuot. Each had 10-12 U.S. Special Forces-led reconnaissance teams, or RTs, along with their 4-6 indigenous hill tribesmen mercenaries.

Indig: Indigenous hill tribesmen from South Vietnam who worked as mercenaries on SOG teams. They were usually Montagnards or Chinese Nungs.

KIA: Killed In Action.

Klick: One kilometer.

KNU: Founded in 1947, the Karen National Union, was created to push for an independent state within Burma where the 7 million Karen people could live in peace. In 1976, they gave up their demands for an independent state. To this day, while a peaceful solution is being sought with the Burmese Regime, the Karen are still subjected to persecution and continued deadly clashes with Burmese forces. Many have escaped Burma and live in villages in the mountains of northern Thailand.

LZ: Landing Zone. Often little more than a patch of barren jungle large enough for a helicopter to hover over while an RT leaped to the ground.

MACVSOG: Military Assistance Command, Vietnam, Special Observation Group. The headquarters for SOG was located in Saigon, South Vietnam.

Montagnard: Referred to as 'yards by Special Forces, Montagnards were ethnic hill tribesman located throughout the Central Highlands of South Vietnam. They were highly regarded for their fighting skills and recruited as mercenaries for SOG teams.

MTT: Mobile Training Team

Nungs: Also hired as mercenaries by SOG, the Nungs were hill tribesmen of Chinese ancestry.

NVA: The North Vietnamese Army

One-Zero: SOG RT team leader.

One-One: SOG RT assistant team leader.

One-Two: SOG RT radio operator.

RON: Remain Over Night. When it was necessary for a team to stay the night in the jungle, a site was chosen in an inaccessible location when possible, usually on the slope of hill deep in the jungle and away from any trail or road.

RPD: A 7.62mm caliber light machine gun of either Russian or Chinese manufacturer. The machine gun was fed by either a metallic link belt holding 50 rounds or a metal drum holding 100 rounds. It was the standard light machine gun utilized by the Viet Cong.

RPG: A portable, shouldered held, rocket propelled grenade launcher capable of propelling a 40mm round to a distance of 500 meters. Fairly accurate, the missile can penetrate up to 12 inches of armor plating.

RPK: Later replaced the RPD and was used by NVA forces.

RT: Reconnaissance, or recon, team. A team usually consisted of 2-3 U.S. Special Forces personnel and 4-6 Montagnards, Nungs, or sometimes, South Vietnamese mercenaries.

SOG: Special Observation Group. SOG was the code word for the covert cross-border units that operated in Laos, Cambodia, and the DMZ.

VC: Viet Cong. The South Vietnamese guerilla forces who were aligned with the NVA to overthrow the South Vietnamese and reunite the country into one under the communist rule of Ho Chi Minh.

WIA: Wounded In Action.

'Yards: Name given to the Montagnards by U.S. forces.